Darkest Need

Also From Rachel Van Dyken

Mafia Royals
Royal Bully
Ruthless Princess
Scandalous Prince
Destructive King
Fallen Royal
Broken Crown

Liars, Inc.
Dirty Exes
Dangerous Exes

Covet Series
Stealing Her
Finding Him

Bro Code Series
Co-Ed
Seducing Mrs. Robinson
Avoiding Temptation
The Set-Up

Elite Bratva Brotherhood
Debase

The Players Game Series
Fraternize
Infraction
MVP

The Consequence Series
The Consequence of Loving Colton
The Consequence of Revenge
The Consequence of Seduction
The Consequence of Rejection

Fall
Eternal
Strung
Capture

The Renwick House Series
The Ugly Duckling Debutante
The Seduction of Sebastian St. James
An Unlikely Alliance
The Redemption of Lord Rawlings
The Devil Duke Takes a Bride

The London Fairy Tales Series
Upon a Midnight Dream
Whispered Music
The Wolf's Pursuit
When Ash Falls

The Seasons of Paleo Series
Savage Winter
Feral Spring

The Wallflower Series (with Leah Sanders)
Waltzing with the Wallflower
Beguiling Bridget
Taming Wilde

The Dark Ones Saga
The Dark Ones
Untouchable Darkness
Dark Surrender
Darkest Temptation
Darkest Sinner

Stand-Alones
Mafia Casanova (with M Robinson)
Hurt: A Collection (with Kristin Vayden and Elyse Faber)
Rip
Compromising Kessen

Darkest Need

A Dark Ones Novella

By Rachel Van Dyken

1001 DARK NIGHTS
PRESS

Darkest Need
By Rachel Van Dyken
Copyright 2023
ISBN: 979-8-88542-029-7

Published by 1001 Dark Nights Press, an imprint of Evil Eye Concepts, Incorporated

Acknowledgments from the Author

I'm going to keep this short and sweet so you can get into one of my favorite stories ever! This was a hard one to write, my emotions were all over the place, but it was so, so fun! I'm so thankful to God that I can write books, and that I'm able to dive deep into fantasy and paranormal lore and create my own world. Liz, Jillian, MJ-thank you so much for taking a chance on me and giving me the privilege to write for 1001 Dark Nights. Jill, thanks for editing super fast and helping me with all of my questions that had to do with Judaism. Husband, two kiddos, thanks for being okay with me holing up in a room so I could finish! You guys are the best and I truly appreciate and love you from the bottom of my heart. Changing diapers while trying to write sexy scenes, not the easiest thing I've ever done haha. Hugs, RVD

One Thousand and One Dark Nights

Once upon a time, in the future...

*I was a student fascinated with stories and learning.
I studied philosophy, poetry, history, the occult, and
the art and science of love and magic. I had a vast
library at my father's home and collected thousands
of volumes of fantastic tales.*

*I learned all about ancient races and bygone
times. About myths and legends and dreams of all
people through the millennium. And the more I read
the stronger my imagination grew until I discovered
that I was able to travel into the stories... to actually
become part of them.*

*I wish I could say that I listened to my teacher
and respected my gift, as I ought to have. If I had, I
would not be telling you this tale now.
But I was foolhardy and confused, showing off
with bravery.*

*One afternoon, curious about the myth of the
Arabian Nights, I traveled back to ancient Persia to
see for myself if it was true that every day Shahryar
(Persian: شهريار, "king") married a new virgin, and then
sent yesterday's wife to be beheaded. It was written
and I had read that by the time he met Scheherazade,
the vizier's daughter, he'd killed one thousand
women.*

*Something went wrong with my efforts. I arrived
in the midst of the story and somehow exchanged
places with Scheherazade – a phenomena that had
never occurred before and that still to this day, I
cannot explain.*

*Now I am trapped in that ancient past. I have
taken on Scheherazade's life and the only way I can
protect myself and stay alive is to do what she did to
protect herself and stay alive.*

*Every night the King calls for me and listens as I spin tales.
And when the evening ends and dawn breaks, I stop at a
point that leaves him breathless and yearning for more.
And so the King spares my life for one more day, so that
he might hear the rest of my dark tale.*

*As soon as I finish a story... I begin a new
one... like the one that you, dear reader, have before
you now.*

Prologue

Tarek

Listen, I know I have chains wrapped strategically around my wrists and that every second that goes by, said chains are burning a mark into my skin that may or may not mean I'm about to get completely demolished by a succubus demon.

But this is not how the story starts.

I mean, maybe it's how it ends since I've been in this exact spot for the last two days without food or water, waiting for a rescue from my immortal friends, knowing full well they're probably all just having sex and enjoying marital bliss without realizing I'm actually missing.

Me.

The manager of the Seattle demon bar, Sin.

Werewolf prince.

All around really upright kind of guy—or so I like to think. But do you know where that got me?

Here.

Chained.

See also: Demon goddess who has not come back to check on me even once and says she wants to kill me via sex.

Bartending is looking great right now. Immortal life in my werewolf clan did not prepare me for this or the fact that saving one succubus would actually turn me into her prey.

She was bruised.

Beaten beyond recognition.

I was going to kill the vampire that attempted to slaughter her, but that's a longer, more violent story since she ended up doing the deed once she got a bit of my blood. But I did give her water, thinking, *wow, I've done this person a total solid*. I mean, despite the fact that she was pretty. Even her tears were pretty. The bruising and swelling on her face didn't even hide how beautiful she was—or *is*.

Maybe my first wrong act was comforting her. Because the minute we touched, her eyes flashed a creepy red, and well…see also *actual* burning handcuffs around my wrists.

It's clearly been a fun forty-eight hours. Maybe she'll make it quick, though a weird part of me kind of wants my last few moments being sucked dry via sex to last for a while, so long that it's all I focus on, all I care about, all I see.

I see visions of the future, but I never saw this.

So, strap in because I'm sure it's going to be a great story. I just may not make it all the way to the end with you.

Chapter One

Tarek

Three Days Prior

"So, a werewolf walks into a bar…" I grin. "Does he actually walk into it, or does the bar walk into him? So many questions, so many answers. Hey, bro." I snap my fingers twice. "You drunk?"

The guy shakes his head once, twice. Oh, wow, we have a goner. I wait until his head hits the table with a giant thud that has me wincing in pain on his behalf, then call for help. "Need a ride here!"

I don't know why I do what I do.

I don't know why I keep working, day after day after freaking day, trying to help the world when I can't even help myself. But here I am. A werewolf created by the gods to just…sit and serve alcohol.

I feel like this would be the part in school where they ask you: *"Hey, what's your passion? What's going to change the world?"*

Me: Beer.

That's my life's purpose, even though I'm second in line for the Earth throne. And before you get all like, *oh, Earth throne, oh, werewolf,* let me get you caught up.

Werewolves aren't weird, and we aren't creepy things that go bump in the night and feed off the world, then howl at the moon. We literally just take care of the Earth and make sure bad juju doesn't happen. Ergo, my brother, who is literally half Fallen Angel and half human and the King of the Soil, aka the Earth. So, what he says goes. All werewolves bow to him and his authority to make sure no bad things come to the world and try to bring on mass destruction via Fallen Angels and immortals fighting against humans. Like the Garden of Eden. Don't even get me started on that fallout.

And then there's me.

Someone who can hear everyone's thoughts, someone who knows I need to protect everything, but also someone without a fucking purpose.

I serve drinks. I help others. I mean, I even helped an old lady with her groceries, and I didn't even growl.

The point is, life is fleeting for humans. Mine, however? Lasts like hundreds of years, and all my friends are married, which sucks. Because, again…time. And now I'm about five seconds away from getting puked on by the guy in front of me.

"It just sucks, bro!" he yells.

"Yes, it does suck a dick." I nod. "Tell me more." My ability to keep a straight face is stellar. I don't even think about it anymore, just nod and smile while words and sometimes puke gets thrown in my direction. It's a gift, what can I say?

"And then she was all like, 'I'll kill you!'" The guy slams his hand against the bar top and looks up as if he can see the Heavens themselves. "All I wanted was a sandwich."

"Violent." I nod in agreement. "Very violent. And I am a fan of sandwiches so I apologize I can't meet your needs right now."

"But, bro…" He wipes another tear from his cheek, then grabs a napkin and blows his nose, tossing the tissue onto the bar. I quickly shove it off and into the trash. "She was right, and I like her violence."

"Maybe"—I lean in—"the journey you need to take is more violent than others. Or maybe she just doesn't like you, bro." She literally does not like him. And I'm beginning to see why.

"No!" He jumps to his feet and thrusts his fist into the air. "I'll fight for her."

"Yay. Go get her," I encourage as he falls to his knees and passes out. "Go, get your woman…man…person—" I pause. "Cricket, spider, demon. Whatever the hell you are—"

"Stop manifesting." Timber, my boss, the actual Egyptian God of the Underworld, shows up next to me with his perfectly pressed navy suit and white-blond hair. Bet he even gets manicures. But I don't want him to smite me, so I say nothing. "It's weird. And also, you can't mate a cricket with a spider. The biology is all off. Just allow him to pass out like a normal human, then phase him out, grab him a car make sure he has only happy memories from your phasing so he comes back to the bar, and then get back to work."

Ah, immortals. Gotta love them. Even when you want to murder them half the time.

"But I hate phasing," I grumble under my breath. "It makes them forget everything, and I feel like shit because they just repeat all their bad choices, and I get to witness it. Oh, shit. It's like *Groundhog Day*. Or is that *Freaky Friday*?"

He sighs. "*Freaky Friday* is where they switch bodies. *Groundhog Day* is where the day goes on repeat. Why am I even engaging in this conversation right now?" He rolls his creepy blue eyes and wraps his knuckles on the bar top. "Phasing is necessary if you want the human to stay sane. They can only handle so much of the nectar we put in our liquor. Plus, who wants to remember puking on the ground and getting accidentally sucked on by a demon?"

"Nobody," I answer truthfully. "I think it even makes you sad, and you have no heart."

"But"—he winks—"thanks to my wife, gorgeous goddess that she is, I do have a soul."

"So do I. But I didn't need to wander in the Egyptian desert for thousands of years to find it. Weren't you on your hands and knees in the sand for years—and years and *years*?"

He growls, "Low blow."

"I like blowing."

"Wow." He checks his watch. "I'm late for dinner. Lock up when you clean up the drunkenness. You're coming over, right? Or are you staying late for guys' night?"

He has a home with a family. I have a grumpy roommate who is still trying to bring himself to understand the modern world. I swear he nearly shat his pants when he saw a microwave. Ancient Gods like Horus need a manual, though he did manage to conquer TikTok.

Home. I wonder what that's really like. Everyone has their person. Did I mention Timber forced Horus to become my roommate so I could help him? But now that Horus has his person, it's just me, all alone in a sad, depressing room. That's why I work late. What's the point of home if you don't truly have one? What's the point of going to an empty room and existing? I've worked for Timber for the last eighteen months, helped save his life, and now I just get to hear people's thoughts, see their futures, and realize I have none.

Wow, shit just got dark.

"Nah, man." I shake my head. "Might go hunt."

"So, you're going to Taco Bell?"

"They give good chalupa." I shrug because nothing sounds more depressing than sitting on the sidewalk outside Taco Bell and people-watching.

He sighs. Yup, I've officially driven Anubis—aka Timber—insane. Feels kind of right, though.

"Please." He grits his teeth. "Phase the passed-out human, go do the job I pay you for, and for the love of the Creator, stop wearing shirts that show off your chest and biceps. It's why we get sued."

"I like my shirts!" I yell.

"So do they." He basically points at every single human and demon in the club. Is it my fault I look good in a nice muscle tee? No, but still, he's the boss and kind of a demon king with a godlike past. So, what he says goes. Last time he got pissed, he burned down his office. I mean, I think it had to do with the sex he was currently having. But still, there was trauma.

I sigh and pick the dude up from the floor. Then, very carefully so as not to be noticed by all the drunk people, I wave a hand over his face. His eyes flash blue before returning to brown. "What just happened?"

"You're really drunk." I pat him on the back. "But I grabbed you a car. Name's Penny, drives a black Ford Focus, and should be here in the next few minutes." I nod to security. They escort him out, and then I return to the rag I've been using to wipe down the bar top.

I swipe and then look to the right, making sure security actually escorted him out.

It's a busy night full of humans dancing with demons they assume are just really good-looking people and have no ill intent, and the drinks are flowing so hard I've already sent home at least a dozen patrons because they couldn't put one foot in front of the other. Timber blames the Ambrosia we put in the liquor. I blame the stupidity on the humans and their inability to know when enough is enough.

The door to the bar opens as security walks back in. Following them in is a girl, stumbling so hard I'm afraid she'll chip a tooth on the hard concrete floor.

Her hair's blue, which is pretty normal for any bar or place downtown. I don't even really notice it, only that it's sticking to her face with something red, and her cheeks are swollen. I squint. It almost looks like she's been beaten. She stumbles toward the bar in her short denim cutoffs, combat boots, and black tank top, then slams her hand onto the bar next to the rag and whimpers.

There's a dagger sticking out of the top of her hand, and her right eye is so swollen she can barely make eye contact with me. Before she stumbles closer, blood trickles down her right arm. She's wearing black fishnet tights with her shorts and the tank is cropped and looks like it's been torn half off. I don't know if it's the look she's going for or if she's been truly attacked—even beyond what I can already see.

I hop over the bar and grab her before she passes out, then carry her into the back office, shoving past everyone dancing. I nod at Timber to take over.

He frowns but returns the gesture as I shove into the office and slam the door closed, laying her on the black leather couch to examine her. That's the good thing about immortals, nothing really fazes us. So if I nod to him, and he nods to me, we both know he'll have my back if shit goes bad. But until then, I'll handle it.

Werewolves can heal others since we're self-healing, but I'm not sure what kind of internal injuries she may have at this point.

"Hey." I grip her face gently. "What's your name?"

She shakes her head, and then it lolls to the side until she's completely passed out.

Well, that's a no-go.

"I'm just going to pull the knife out of your hand," I say to myself and wince when blood surges from her wound. I toss the dagger onto the floor and grip her palm between mine. My skin burns where I touch her. The weapon looks familiar, but I can't figure out why as I continue to hold her hand tightly. The stab wound was deep—very deep.

I feel my eyes flash blue as I heal the wound, knitting the skin back together, but then I can't let go. I start to pull away. How is her grip so strong when she's not even conscious?

I tug again.

Her grip only tightens until her eyes flash open. They're blood-red. She pulls me with inhuman strength right onto her bloody chest.

Her eyes don't just lock onto mine. They hold me captive in a near chokehold around my body, suffocating me and pulling me closer and closer.

Despite her swollen face, she grips the back of my neck and pulls me in for a soul-sucking kiss.

I freeze, feeling my energy leaving my body. The last thing I remember is thinking, *huh, so this is how it ends.*

Death by kiss.

And then everything goes painfully black.

Chapter Two

Lilith

He tastes like a dream. The really good kind that you want to keep experiencing over and over again and maybe never wake up from because the pain of reality is too suffocating.

I know I should stop, but I just can't. I want to taste him, suck him dry…again and again.

He's asleep. They always are. It's the effect of the venom I release when I start to suck. It actually pushes into their bodies and makes them go limp so I can do what I need to do.

Feed.

Like a spider attacking its prey and paralyzing them.

I remember the first time. I was sixteen and saw the hot chem teacher I had a crush on. I walked up to him, and he just…gave in. The janitor's closet was never the same, and not because I had some crazy sexual experience, but because the guy's body lacked any blood once I was done. It started seeping out under the door and running down the hallway.

This one tastes different than a human. He's also pretty. Plus, he's helping me… I kind of want to keep him for a while and see where things go in the next few days.

Normally, it takes twenty-four hours for me to feed on a human. If they're immortal, it takes at least three days. But this guy…

He's different. I wonder how he would handle it, and I also want to know what would happen to me if I tried.

So different. I inhale and press my mouth against his neck. Why does it feel this way?

"That tickles." His gruff whisper has me jerking back. "But I kind of like it."

"What?" I wave a hand in front of his face. What's happening? "How are you even awake right now?"

"Because I'm amazing, and I just needed a fucking nap. Why are you sniffing my neck? And why the hell are you trying to suck me dry? That's not even polite. At least, ask first. I think the conversation goes a little like this: '*Oh, hi, I'm a succubus. I might suck your…bus*'—haha. Okay, sorry, still delirious—and then you go on to do your thing. I do my thing and pretend to be asleep, and then you get your earth energy or whatever the hell they call it, and we go our separate ways. PS, I will not be your slave. I do not do well being told what to do. I'm more of a manager sort of person. *I* like to tell people what to do. But if it gets your kink on, I'm okay for the next"—he checks his watch—"five minutes. Then, I'm out."

"Who are you?" I shake my head in disbelief. This has seriously never happened before. Granted, I control my need for blood and energy better now that I'm almost thirty, but he should literally be either dead or passed out for days. And I shouldn't already be healing.

"Tarek." His name sounds familiar. "Werewolf prince, all around badass, reads minds—except yours is frighteningly closed off. May need to work on that. So, are we good here? Can I go?" He starts to get up.

I push him back onto the couch. "I've never—"

"Let me save you words. I know, blah blah blah, you've never had anyone break the succubus demon spell. But here's the thing. I'm not like you. I'm different. Special, if you will. So, if you don't need any more of my energy to survive, I'm just gonna go out the front door. There *is* a front door, right?" He rubs his eyes. "See? I'm delirious. Not the front door, I mean the office door." He yawns and stretches his arms over his head, giving me a beautiful view of his golden abs. Seriously, who is this guy? His body is massive lying on the couch.

I literally have no words. My mouth dry, I point to the door.

He nods. "Thanks."

He gets his massive body off the leather couch and stretches again. "Do you know any good bagel places around here?"

Doesn't he work here? Did I make him stupid? "I don't understand."

"Bagels. As in bread that looks like a circle with a hole in the middle of—"

"I know what a bagel is!" I yell, frustrated with how nonchalant he is. "But how are you…? Why are you…? I don't get it. Plus, this city is your home. I just moved from Portland before I got attacked."

He pauses. "Life, man. So confusing." He pats me on the arm, followed by the head, then sidesteps me. "The mysteries of the universe just keep on hitting, am I right? All right, then." Did he just pat me on the head and then wipe his hand on his shirt like my hair's dirty? I mean, I guess it probably is since I was just attacked. God, I don't even want to know how rough I look right now. But seriously, what in the ever-loving hell? I just got it dyed before my attack in the alleyway. And I wasn't even doing anything wrong, just hunting a weak vampire I thought I could take on to last me another few days before I figured out what to do with my life. All I remember is walking. I don't even know why I was walking in that direction. I hate that my memories make no sense, just as much as I hate what I am.

"Anyway."

"Wait." I hold out my hand.

At least I'm not bleeding anymore; that's nice. And he *did* heal my knife wound. Why was I even stabbed in the first place?

I can feel Earth energy from feeding off Tarek, but it feels different, not right. Though not wrong, either. It feels purposeful in a way that makes me hesitant.

I stare down at my shaky hands. "What sort of werewolf are you?"

He leans down slowly until we're face-to-face. "The very best kind." He winks. "The kind I imagine you'd want to feed off of for an eternity. But I have beer to serve, so I'll just be going now."

"Halt!" I yell.

He smirks over his shoulder. "Did you seriously just say, '*halt?*'"

"It was the first thing that came to my mind."

"Really? The very first thing? How old are you, anyway? That's such an old word to use to say—" He shakes his head and then freezes. "Um, please tell me I didn't see what I just saw."

"What?"

He sniffs the air and then ignores me completely, walking out of the office and right up to the vampire who attacked me. Brave guy to stop at the bar I ran into. "You."

The vampire starts laughing. "Me? Do we know each other?" He tries to walk past Tarek. "I'm just here for a drink. Had a rough night."

He's younger, which doesn't mean stronger, despite what you may have read. But he can still terrorize the entire bar and create a huge mess, and all because he followed me in for a beer.

He has jet-black hair, vibrant green eyes, and is the exact same height and build as the werewolf.

This will not end well.

Still, I stand behind Tarek. I can hold my own, but not against an immortal like the vampire. I'm not strong enough, and since I can feel the werewolf blood in me, I know he has to be stronger than I am. Maybe he's part of the Council? Maybe he's just really old. Demons aren't necessarily a race of powerful immortals unless we feed or have souls.

I have no soul.

And I only fed enough to heal my body.

How depressing.

I wouldn't last longer than an hour, and by then, the vampire would be the one doing the biting, and I'd be the one doing the dying.

Sometimes, it sucks that your only power is to seduce and consume, and that bagels, as this weird werewolf said, don't even cure the hunger or need.

"You need to leave." Hot werewolf who goes by the name of Tarek crosses his bulky arms over his tight black T-shirt and clenches his teeth. Why does a man bun and his caramel-colored hair look so good on him? Why is he so good-looking? Why does he smell and taste good, like earth energy? Life?

Why do I always feel like I taste like death?

I swallow the lump in my throat and self-consciously rub my sticky arms, still standing behind Tarek when I feel a presence.

I'm almost afraid to turn.

The hairs on the back of my arms rise, and I suddenly feel something else—something bigger, stronger. What the hell is happening?

The door behind the vampire, the one to enter the bar, opens. Music still kills my ears, lights are everywhere, people are dancing, and then I see a flash of…it.

I scramble more behind the werewolf and grip him tightly. "D-Dark One. There's a Dark One. The king—I think the King of the Immortals."

A low voice rumbles behind me, whispering, "Don't let him hear that, he has quite the ego."

I slowly look over my shoulder into crisp, gorgeous blue eyes. They flash red before going back to normal.

I know exactly who this is.

Rumors of his resurrection have run rampant. According to all the immortals I know, the Fallen Gods were resurrected, and the Fallen Angels are on the same side.

And the Creator has allowed it to set everyone free from the Fall.

I just didn't realize the place I'd moved to would have them living here and in the flesh. Wait, did I move? Where do I even live? And why am I so confused? Maybe the attack. Yeah, I'm in shock. Total shock. That's it.

The Egyptian god reaches out and touches my cheek, tilting his head curiously. "So, you're her. Interesting. And here I thought this week would be boring. Sucked a little werewolf, did you now?"

"I was hurt." I try not to stumble over my words as I hold on to the werewolf. "I didn't know who he was, or that you were here, or that the King of the Immortals was...here."

I've never been more terrified in my entire existence. I think. How old am I again?

He lifts my chin with his thumb. "I think I'll enjoy this."

I close my eyes in dread. He's seconds away from killing me.

"Cassius," he barks. "Take care of the trash. We don't allow vampires who feed on innocents in my club, and I would really hate to spread blood everywhere before dinner. I'll escort him to..." He walks up to the vampire, who suddenly stumbles back. "Where he belongs."

Cassius smirks from behind the vampire. "And you do know where you belong when you harm any of the immortals here—or humans, for that matter."

"Look, man..." The guy spreads his hands wide. He's shaking. "I don't want any trouble. Had I known she was under the Council's immortal protection, I wouldn't have—"

"Should have never," Timber—or his god name, Anubis—answers.

"Not even once," Cassius agrees. "We have rules here in Seattle, in this club, and you know, just in general. Right, Prince Tarek?"

So that's why. Makes sense. He's one of them. I was right. He's most likely on the Council, and if he's a prince, then he's second to only the King of the Werewolves, which means he's old.

Tarek just grins. "Guys, you know I had this."

"Why does everyone have fun without me?" A voice sounds as someone kicks the door open, revealing basically the most gorgeous man alive—a male siren. Oh, perfect. I now have most of the Immortal Council in front of me. He's been known to seduce anything that breathes. Bet he tastes good, too. He's married, though, and has the blood of a god in him—Ra, to be specific. Apparently, none of the Egyptian gods actually died, they just started an immortal race.

There are too many powerful people here to count. Sirens. Werewolves. Angels. Gods—

And they just keep coming.

Literally.

"What does it take to get a good drink around here?" The door opens again, revealing…wow. Yeah, basically the King of the Vampires. Long, jet-black hair, green eyes, leather jacket with a bloody shirt beneath it, and married with twins and another on the way.

All of it checks out.

I am in actual Immortal Hell.

Cassius. Mason. Tarek. Timber. Ethan. And our resident siren, Alex. Not to mention Stephanie and a few others. The Immortal Council, the ones in charge of making sure humans across the world are protected. The ones who work for the Creator. The ones who've protected our entire species from the Fallen.

The only stories I know are the ones I've picked up from people who took pity on me after my parents' deaths.

But they're legends.

I feel like I'm about to pass out.

Ethan sighs. "And one of my own. Unbelievable. You know, you just want one night out without responsibility."

Alex grins. "Yes, because being a parent is so hard."

"Damn." Mason chuckles under his breath. "Timber's bar may never be the same after that comment."

Ethan lunges. Alex grins, and Cassius just rolls his eyes as if he's been dealing with toddlers—aka the Immortal Council—for longer than he can remember. He slowly whispers, "Stop."

The entire room freezes, except for our little get-together. Everyone is literally frozen in time, save for the tiny pieces of dust in the air that slowly fall all around us.

"Alex, I swear. If you don't stop pestering him, I will make you ash."

Alex grins. "I live for it."

"And yet you might die from it," Cassius growls and spreads his arms wide, feathers shooting from his back to form giant, purple and blue wings. I stumble backward. He plucks a feather and very slowly brings it to the vampire's neck. "We don't harm others unless they truly deserve Hell. Do you understand?"

His pulse races; I can sense it with how my mouth waters. Tarek slowly pulls me to his side and keeps me there as if he knows I'm tempted to get my revenge and drink all the vampire's energy but am too terrified to get close to Cassius to do so.

"I think we should let her," Tarek says. "Let her take what he stole."

Cassius nods his head. "And the rest of you?"

"If it makes it go faster," Ethan grumbles. "You, Alex?"

"Blood." Alex sighs. "So messy. Plus, Mason's already behind the bar pouring drinks because we're taking too long, bro." He looks at Tarek. "Don't you work here?"

Timber sighs. "I'll go help. You guys deal with this. Don't make a mess, and let me know when I need to guide him to the Underworld. Haven't been in a few months. Kind of miss—" He stops talking. "My brother." And now, this is where I faint as Horus, God of the Sky, just nonchalantly walks into the bar with his bleach-blond hair, gorgeous, chiseled face, ripped jeans, and no shirt.

Timber points at the sign. "No shirt, no service."

Horus walks over to one of the frozen dancing humans, grabs the guy's shirt from him, and puts it on. "Better?"

"Animal." Timber laughs.

Horus just shrugs. "What sort of party am I missing? I thought it was weekly guys' night. I've been busy, and that vampire looks ready to shit his pants. You good, bro?"

The vampire who attacked me actually starts peeing himself. I almost laugh, except I'm also terrified. I can't look away from the tattoo on Horus's face that tells everyone in existence just how powerful he is, *what* he is, and what he's capable of.

"I think…" Cassius locks eyes with me. "I say we let her have some fun, take back what was stolen, and go have a drink."

"Yup." The rest of them walk by.

All but Horus, who stops by my side and leans down at least a foot and a half. "Break his heart, and I'll break you."

I start to shake. "T-the vampire?"

His lips are so close to my ear I can feel the heat from them. "No. The werewolf. Trust me when I say he's more tender than you think, and he's like my brother. Mark my words, if you harm him, you won't even remember getting your limbs ripped from your body." He squeezes my shoulder and walks off. "What beer's on tap?"

Tarek sighs next to me, still holding me. "He's been very dramatic since he found out his wife is pregnant. Don't worry, he doesn't bite—I mean, not like Ethan does. Or me. I don't think my bite is extremely hard in general, but—" I point at the vampire trying to escape through the door. "Oh, sorry. Yeah, be right back. But"—he backs up—"before I catch him, do you like, want him dead before or after you suck? I can prepare him any way. Might have been a chef in another life, who knows?"

My jaw drops. "Um."

"Never mind." God, his wink is gorgeous. "Be right back. Grab a napkin because you're about to suck him dry—compliments of the chef."

I barely see him move through the open door before he's back, and the vampire's on his knees in front of me, getting drug through the bar and into the back office.

I follow, slowly.

Tarek releases him, then hits him across the face to make sure he's out. "All yours, pretty little demon. Better you feed on him than me."

"Why's that?" I ask in a small voice.

Tarek leans down until we're face-to-face. "Because at the end of the day, I truly don't think you can handle me, little girl." He pats me on the head and shuts the door, only to crack it open again. "Oh, and try not to make a mess. I really like my couch."

Chapter Three

Tarek

"Don't." I wipe the bar top. "Timber left to go hang out with his wife after one drink since he literally can't get drunk unless it's off her, and you guys are all staring at me like I have a billion heads."

Cassius is the first to lean back in his chair, arms crossed in his perfectly pressed suit and looking pissed—like he does at least ninety percent of the time. Or maybe he's just perplexed about how he ended up with the job of taking care of all of us *and* humanity. Jury's still out. "Did she really suck on you?"

Alex chokes on his beer and looks away, wiping a small drip from his chin. "I feel like that's a super personal question to ask, but I, too, want to know what happened. And not that I'm like, *hey, give us details*, but also..." He leans in with a grin. "Give us details. Feel free to leave nothing out."

"Three." Ethan chimes in.

"Four," Mason says from behind me.

"Oh, yeah." Horus holds up his hand. "Five. Sorry, forgot to have an opinion. But you know, this could be good for you, give up the TikTok, dating apps, the constant one-night stands where you bang against the wall over and over again, and I wake up to screaming—" He looks up. "Sorry, was that an overshare? I forget sometimes." He stares at all the expressions of annoyance, mine included. "Oh, please. I've been in modern times for like a year. I get a free pass. You know, like when you play Monopoly." He waves us off.

Ethan sighs. "You know we can't play anymore now that we're all married, and the women are too competitive. I lost so many properties last time, and dumbshit over there just threw the board."

He's pointing at me.

I'm the dumbshit.

I take a deep breath. "It's because I didn't have a partner and felt tag-teamed."

Because I don't have one.

I don't see one in my future, either.

How bad does it suck when you see everyone else's, but when you look into yours, it's like this dark abyss?

Everyone starts laughing. I smile, but internally, I wonder. I hate wondering what the universe has planned for me. Not only is it frustrating, but apparently, the only action I get are the women I take home from the bar or ones who attack me for trying to help them.

Though it would have been a nice way to go. Her bite was deep, my dick was hard, and she smelled incredible.

All part of the charm until you get sucked dry.

I shake it off. "No more game-night talk. You guys finish your drinks. I'll check on the most-likely-dead vampire. Since Timber left, someone else gets the honor of sending his body where it belongs. And I swear if she got blood anywhere, I'm committing murder."

Ethan smirks. "Why in the hell are you so attached to that couch?"

I don't tell him it's the only piece of furniture I have from Scotland, my actual home. I don't tell any of them I'm homesick or that my heart feels like it's constantly bleeding for something it doesn't know it needs.

I can't tell them I feel isolated while surrounded by others.

Or that, sometimes, I wonder what the point is when we're all truly alone at the end of the day.

"Dad!" I screamed. "Let him stay! He's my brother!"

My dad glared at me. "He's an abomination."

A tear slid down my cheek as Mason slowly gave me his back and hung his head. "I just wanted to check in one last time. Wanted to let you know I'm thriving under the Dark One. Tell you I have a purpose. I wanted…"

I wait for what he'll say.

Under his breath, he whispered, "Christmas."

My soul died inside my body. It was one of our favorite holidays. He had been cast out centuries ago, and all I wanted was to have my brother by my side. Instead, he'd been abandoned—even though he was the heir to the throne, given to my father by the Creator of all things.

"Mason!" I yelled, reaching for him.

He shook his head and walked away.

I have only two memories of this past: one where I see into it and witness what my parents did to save him—they gave him Fallen Angel blood to keep him alive. And the second…

Christmas.

Sometimes, I wonder why my nightmares always repeat. Other times, I know it's probably because of my abilities.

When I asked my parents why I had the gift, they went completely silent.

I still don't know why the question was a big deal. I have no clue. All I know is that I have something most werewolves don't, and for whatever reason, it makes me a sort of outlier, even though I'm a prince.

"Hey." Mason hits me in the arm. "Why do you look like you're ready to cry?"

"Huh?" I feel like time just escaped me, as if I'm not myself. "Meh. Maybe it's because a succubus took advantage of me sexually on my favorite couch. But whatever, I'm over it."

Alex laughs and takes another sip of his beer. "Or were you on it, and she was on you? I just feel like we need to experience the whole seduction. God knows it's my specialty."

Cassius sighs. "It's weird when an immortal's immaturity goes in reverse. So very strange."

Timber holds up his hand for a high five, and Cassius actually hits it.

"See," I point out. "To me, that's weird. Anubis and an angel, high-fiving. Like that's not even remotely normal."

Cassius frowns. "Aren't high fives a way to show solidarity?"

"Yeah." Ethan nods.

"Then…" He high-fives Timber again. "See what I did there? That's called bonding, communication, and not making my job harder. Well done, God of the Underworld. You can sit at my table."

Alex shakes his head. "Never thought I'd see the fucking day."

"Because of all the sex?" Horus nods.

"Someone, anyone." I raise my hand. "Take away his ability to be on social media. It's really corrupting his old, old, so *very* old…ancient, might I add? Mind."

She returns on that note, staring between all of us, then plops down on a barstool. "Yeah, he's probably dead. By the way, my name's Lilith if you wanted to report it to the police, but a lot of good it would do since you guys are who you are."

"Yeah, he's probably dead."

"Up top!" Alex raises his hand.

Horus leans into me. "Do we celebrate death now?"

"Shhhhhh." I bat him away. "They're bonding over the high five."

Lilith nods, wipes her face again, and then looks around the table. "I have to say, I didn't expect you guys to be like…normal."

Ethan bursts out laughing, which is rare for him. "Oh, sorry. I thought that was a joke."

"At least I understand sarcasm now." Cassius laughs. "All right, so now that we've saved the world from the bad vampire and have a succubus, should we do a toast?"

"A toast?" Lilith asks. "I don't think I've ever made a toast with…" She gulps and spreads her arms wide. "This. These kinds of…humans—immortals—people. Beings?"

Alex shakes his head. "It's like a baby lamb. Can I keep it?"

"No!" we all yell in unison.

"She isn't a pet, you dumbass," I grumble under my breath, and for no reason at all, start to feel my blood heating beneath my skin. "She's—she's…" A vision suddenly appears. I feel my eyes go dark again, like they do when I see the future.

And for once.

I see my own.

Including my end.

Chapter Four

Lilith

Tarek says nothing for the rest of the night. In fact, he's weirdly quiet. We have a few drinks, though nobody can actually get drunk. Which sucks for them because I'm feeling it hard since I've never actually gone shot for shot with a siren, an angel, a werewolf—god? Angel? Have I lost count already?

I grin.

"All right." Tarek pulls me against him. "Let's get you home."

"'Kay." I grin up at him. "You're pretty."

"If I had a nickel…" He winks. His eyes really are so freaking pretty. I get lost in them and look over and over again as I lean against his warm, thick chest. Staring at his full mouth and tempting lips. "What?"

"I'm…" Going to take him. I'm going to take him. Why can't I have nice things? I've been told to hold myself back my entire life, and only from the random people I've met in life that recognized what and who I was and why I needed help. Including my adoptive parents, who, at the time, just looked at me and said to stop the thirst.

But I thirst so badly.

I thirst for him.

My gaze moves to the pulse in his neck. "Can I drink?" I ask politely, maybe I slur it. I don't even know.

He frowns. "You're a demon, not a vampire. But if you need blood?" He nods and bites into his wrist without hesitation while waiting for my ride to show up.

I look down.

Nobody's on the street; I would sense them.

And, apparently, no brain cells exist in my body. His blood is different—*he's* different. Maybe he doesn't even know it. Maybe he does. But the temptation is so strong I don't think a million vampires could keep me from licking him from head to toe.

"Do it," a voice whispers. "Take him. It's your future. Take the Prince of the Earth. Take part of it for yourself."

I stumble back, hands shaking, then stare at his wrist again.

I know him.

I know him well.

I know his…

I feel my body start to weaken…

And then I see it.

His end. My beginning. Maybe it's both. Maybe it's a combination of everything, but I couldn't have prepared for it.

Oh, God.

It's everything.

It's us.

I remember holding his hand.

I remember the Garden.

The apple. And then I remember walking with him.

Red rain fell from the sky.

And she saved us. Eva saved us.

And so began…Genesis.

Chapter Five

Tarek

Pompeii
79 A.D.

It was a bloodbath, plain and simple. It was destruction after destruction, the air filled with red.

"Please," I begged. "Mom. Dad." Did I even have parents? That was an unanswered question. Why did my hands feel so warm? And why did I feel my blood in my veins as if *They* were speaking to me, moving through me? Communicating with me. "Please." Tears burned my cheeks. "Please, just…help." I raised my hand to the Heavens. Raised it so high my shoulder burned. My arm refused to come down.

I needed a savior.

And I had none.

People ran around us, and the mountain continued to erupt and billow smoke until I saw red.

So much that I couldn't fathom it.

Where were my parents? Where was I?

The tears continued to burn my cheeks. They pressed a scar of trauma against my skin that would never go away until I saw her.

I inhaled.

The air was full of smoke. It was messy and burned my throat, but I knew I wasn't gone yet.

Her eyes were full of joy and happiness, and her soul…somehow, I could see it. I could see the blue through her chest, and I knew.

She was good.

I knew it was good.

And I knew…

I would survive this, for whatever purpose it may be. I had no more fear, no more doubts. I reached out my hand. Even at eight years old and with no memories, I reached for my angel.

And she held on.

So much was going on around me. There was so much fire, so much destruction, so much I couldn't comprehend. And then I saw him.

He was clothed in wings of white and gold, dripping with black and white blood.

His gold armor glistened, and he ripped his giant helmet from his face and slammed it against the now-crumbled concrete.

A warm hand grabbed mine. She leaned down, and I saw that her eyes were green, and her hair was black. She squeezed harder, then pulled me to her side. "Don't be afraid, little one."

"Who are you?" I asked.

"Eva. Or you can call me by the name given to me by the Creator. Eve." She smiled again. She looked so pretty with her dark cloak—it had a tree clasp made of real gold around the front. And her skin seemed to glow. "We're going to save you."

"Who?" I asked, looking around.

She reached for another person. Someone I'd been running after in order to get free. The girl had weird dark hair and light eyes.

Eve pulled her into our embrace. "All of you."

"You can't save us from this," the girl whispered and started crying so hard I was afraid she would choke. "Only we can save ourselves. Only we get a few days. Only we know what happens—"

"Shhhh." Eve held her close, pressing the pretty girl's face to her chest. "I save to provide, I save to forgive myself and others, and we save." She looked up. "To protect the world." A tear slid down her cheek. "We save because, what's the point…in abandonment or surrender in this life or the next?"

All I remember is Eve's smell and the girl's. I remember the way the girl stared at me with hope in her eyes.

Hope.

Destiny.

Life.

The man with the armor had a terrifying, deep voice. He looked at us like we were abominations—as if we shouldn't exist. "Do not make me destroy you, vampire!" He yelled it so loudly I covered my ears and screamed.

But the girl, the one who looked about my age, grabbed one of my fingers and then another until we were holding hands, listening to him yell.

I was finally at peace. I was myself. I was here with someone who understood the confusion of being lost, isolated, and abandoned in a burning city.

In a life that didn't make sense.

"One day," she whispered in a shaky voice, her face covered in ash. "I'll tell you."

"What?" I said right back, my lips trembling, my blood boiling to a degree that made no sense, and my teeth elongating as if I needed to eat when I had no idea what I even ate to survive. "Tell me what?"

"It's a prophecy. I'm confused. I can't say." Her frown proved it. "All I know is…savior. A savior. You'll see things, you'll hear. Don't be afraid." She pulled me into her arms and gripped me so tightly I lost my breath, then whispered in a strong voice, "Fear is not welcome here."

Eve stood between us and the menacing man. Her eyes were closed like she was sad, but I thought she was praying, begging, doing anything she could.

To save us. To save more. To become… I slowly frowned. To become.

Dead?

To live out her future.

I touched her hand and whimpered again.

She was killing herself and knew it. For us.

"Cassius, most of them are innocent. Will you destroy them? The children? The mothers? The grandmothers?"

"If I let one go free, one infected with the blend of angelic and demon blood, the end could be catastrophic…"

"Then choose, Cassius," Eve said in a challenging voice. "Choose who goes free, save a few. All I ask is that you save some."

"You misjudge our relationship, vampire," he hissed as if he might kill her at any minute. Even his hands flexed like he was ready to strangle her. The air took on a bitter taste, and he hesitated. I'd never seen an angel before, but I imagined hesitation wasn't a normal thing for them. "Only you would ask this of me. Notice how the rest of the Council members have already fled the city. Yet here you stand."

She lifted her head, her green eyes locking with his. "Here I stand."

"Damn it, woman." He screamed it so loudly I quickly covered my ears and then wanted to cover my eyes for a few brief seconds. He stood tall and stared her down, his expression unreadable. Then, within seconds, a sliver of humanity seemed to slip through. He broke their connection, and his gaze landed on me.

I wonder how it burned, knowing you had to make a choice.

I kept hold of the girl's hand, squeezing it too hard but needing the comfort.

And I kept watching Eve's face to see what would happen.

"I have…" the tall man started. "Less humanity left than you think." His eyes welled with tears. "I will fall. Do you understand, Eve? I will fall. For them, I will fucking fall!"

"Then fall," she said in a calm voice. "Fall for the Creator, fall for us. But mainly, fall for them." She pointed at us. "Fall for the children. Fall for what you believe in. But, Cassius, look at me right now."

His eyes locked with hers. "You will regret it if you do not do this. They are children. They are immortal children. They are special, and they are the reason we are here. We save them, and we save the world from darkness, don't you see?" Tears of red ran down her face. "We fall for them? We fall together. We go to the Underworld, we meet Anubis, we rest. But who's going to save them? We are both hero and destroyer. We were given one task since the Fall. So, if we fall with them? So. Be. It."

"Twelve," he choked out. "I will save twelve."

Eva bowed her dark head. "Thank you, Cassius."

As she walked away from him, he whispered, "This will not be forgotten…daughter of Lilith and son of Enoch."

Chapter Six

Lilith

Present Day

"Where am I?" a low voice asks.

I jump awake and look down at myself. I have blood running down my wrists and am lying with Tarek on a mattress in a place I don't recognize.

But all I see is his blood. All I feel is anger and need and lust. Then there are the memories I don't recognize, ones that don't make sense. It feels so real, like I'm still there right now, watching the boy, watching the world burn around me, and feeling like I might die with it.

Son of Enoch?

Who was the son of Enoch, and why couldn't I remember him? And why the hell am I bleeding so much?

I check my wrists again and then my arms. Wait, that's not my blood. None of it is. And my wrists have no markings.

I jerk around to look at Tarek, realizing exactly what the source is. He has small bites all over his body, down his arms and up his neck. A small trickle of blood runs from his mouth.

He's awake but pale.

"I don't feel the desire to repeat myself, Lilith. Where am I?" He's literally handcuffed to the bed. Did I do that?

I quickly get to my feet and stumble toward him. When I get to the mattress, I notice how his jeans are ripped, along with what had been a whole black T-shirt. It's now shredded, like someone took their fingers and tried to tear it open.

"That is a very long pause for a simple answer." He sighs as if he's not injured or chained to a headboard. "If you could just tell me where I am, I can visualize my escape much easier. Gotta hand it to you; your bite is strong. I didn't realize my blood would make you feral since you weren't injured anymore. But…" He tugs against the handcuffs anchored above his head. They make a jangling noise. "Apparently, you want to keep me as a special treat. I wonder when my life turned from feeding to being fed on. Oh, yes, the minute I tried to get you a car. Did not see that coming. You know, they should really be more random with their bingo cards this year. If *anyone* was going to be chained to a bed, I had Alex down…damn it."

"Stop talking." My voice is hoarse, almost like I've been screaming. But I can't focus on anything but his smooth skin. A full-on, in-real-life eight-pack with lean muscle stacked upon lean muscle, and finally, his ripped jeans, giving me the perfect view of the notorious werewolf thighs. Rumor has it women beg to be trapped between them for life because they're—I shake my head and look down at my trembling hands.

It's happening again, then.

I won't survive this, and neither will he.

Now that I have enough blood in my system and have fed, I realize my current state of reality, and it's not looking good for either of us.

I'll need to consume. I won't be able to stop. I'll remember the next few days like a distant life I lived at one point. And then I'll wake up in another random town and do it all over again.

Two days of ultimate power.

Two days with a werewolf prince.

And he says his bingo card is off.

My only goal is to survive. Now, I have to survive with him.

I sigh. "I didn't bring you here. I merely brought you to her, like I do every time. Now, I'm trapped just as much as you are."

Feminine laughter echoes in the dark room—the same as always with its high ceilings, castle-like vibes, a roaring fireplace in the corner, no windows, enough food, wine, and water piled onto the far wooden table to feed multiple people, and the bed.

There's always the mattress.

I stare at the white velvet blanket just barely covering it and the blood staining parts of it. Everything's the same, right down to the fact that it drips off into the very cup I always provide, sitting right next to the leg—the artery, if I'm being specific.

It's a nightmare I'll always relive, and now I've brought my savior into it.

"You did well this time." She cackles in the dark. "I mean, you do well every time, Daughter of Discord."

I hate being referred to as that. I don't create chaos. I just want to live.

The first time this voice came into my life, I thought I was going crazy. And then she appeared in front of me and told me I was special, even used my name a few times, then finally just laughed and said I was Discord.

I have no idea what that means, but it makes my head spin. I know that once he's completely dry of blood, every single damn memory will come back. I'll most likely hate myself and will continue to hate her, and then I'll be just like Cain, forced to walk the Earth as eternal punishment I never deserved. He did. I don't.

"Well, that's just perfect." Tarek sighs behind me. "Daughter of Discord? Do you know any of your mythology? How old are you?"

The voice laughs. "Oh, my. I knew this would be entertaining. Have I not warned all of you immortals about the strings I like to pull? Big, strapping puppets I can manipulate with my will. By the way, thank you for taking care of Thomas, the vampire who attacked our little Lilith here. He was getting on my nerves and hunting down my favorite puppets of all, and I *do* hate getting bored."

"So, I'm chained to a bed, and a psychopath refuses to show herself. Just talks like this booming voice. Oh, right. You're probably ugly. That actually makes sense."

I jerk my head toward him, then clap a hand over his mouth. I swear the guy needs to keep his thoughts inside his head. "She'll kill us both. Not that you aren't already dead, but I'd like to at least enjoy you before you die."

Tarek's brown eyes glow blue. "I wouldn't be so sure about my death. All I see in my future is darkness. All"—he frowns—"all I see is…" His eyes flash brighter. "Discord. But when I look further…" He strains against his handcuffs, muscles flexing and jaw clenching as he looks into my eyes as if he can see the past, present, and the future. "You." His voice lowers. "You will either be the savior or destroyer of all, and if you take too much of my blood, we both know what will happen."

"What if it saves me?" I sound like I'm begging, but I know she'll kill him anyway. She'll make sure I stay under her spell and need to survive, since the beginning and history will repeat itself. It's always the same.

I took enough of his blood to remember most of it. I was clearly in a frenzy to regain everything, only to destroy it all over again.

Suddenly, I can't breathe.

"Ugly?" She laughs. "Ugly?" I hear her footsteps—one, two, three—her heels clicking against the concrete floor. She's angry. She always gets angry if anyone insults her beauty.

Always.

She says it's a punishment for beginning a war I don't remember starting. Says I begged her to save me after the gods made bets on me. But I don't recall what war—she won't allow it—and I don't know which gods.

Why can I remember my first bite at sixteen and killing a teacher? Why can I remember that I'm forced to fully feed on an immortal once a year to regain any semblance of power that was given to me?

And why does it always go away, only to repeat?

Her footsteps near. I struggle to get close to Tarek.

He shoots me a glare. "Yes, because I could be of so much help to you right now."

"Can't you shift into something?" I whisper under my breath.

He glares harder. "Yes, Lilith, let me just shift my way into wolf mode so my paws—which would be triple the size of my hands, by the way—get caught, as well. I'm strong, but whatever evil witch put me here realizes I can't use my strength when I've been here for God knows how long, getting sucked dry. Not that it matters, because I'm probably already dead. I don't even know if I *can* shift right now because you…" He shakes his head. "You have taken half my blood supply."

I self-consciously wipe my mouth with the back of my hand. "It wasn't on purpose."

"I've been kidnapped, and it wasn't on *purpose*?" He rolls his eyes. "Cool story, tell me more. And…oh, wow"—he looks behind me—"guess you aren't a troll."

Jealousy slams into me as I push his chest to keep some distance between them and then turn around, blocking her from seeing him.

Danu, Goddess of the Earth. The stories have it wrong, and she loves that. She loves that I'm one of the first women on Earth, and she can control me. She loves that she can steal my power because of it.

She lets me feed under my curse, only to suck me dry and force me into servitude over the war.

Her eyes are black, her hair a whitish-blond, and every being who sees her immediately falls for her looks. It doesn't matter that her voice sounds like evil itself. Her pretty face, the one given to her by the Creator, is beautiful, save for one small knife scar from the very one who created her as a warning not to step outside what They allow her to be in control of: watching over the other goddesses and keeping her realm in check, all while wandering the Earth for her sins.

But the Creator isn't here.

It's just me.

Danu leans down and presses a kiss to my cheek. I immediately want to wipe off the blood-red lipstick; instead, I stare up at her, shaking like the weak, addicted person I am. "You should continue your feeding, little succubus."

"I wasn't always a succubus." I lift my chin and try to look strong when I know I'm so weak—*so* weak.

Danu laughs and pats me on the head. "Then maybe don't piss off the Greek gods next time. They like games, not wars, you idiot." She slowly reveals her right hand from inside her cloak.

She's holding a golden apple.

My apple.

The one used in the Garden.

The same one used in...

"Well, shit," Tarek says out of nowhere. "Please, don't tell me that's the relic from the Garden of Eden, which means it's the same one from the Trojan War."

"Shit," I repeat.

"An apple a day." Danu winks and waves the fruit in front of me. "I'm sure by sucking him dry, you'll regain all your fun little goddess powers." She presses a finger to my forehead and then flicks it against my skin. "But you won't have enough time to enjoy them. You caused the Fall. You caused a war. You will always be Discord, and I will always be the one to keep you under control. We all have our curses. And you, Eris, embodiment of Lilith, are mine."

Chapter Seven

Cassius

Greece 79 A.D.

I followed her scent. If things got out of hand, I would stop her at all costs. She'd promised.

She'd lied.

Again.

I wanted to turn a blind eye, mainly because the world didn't feel as dark or desperate when Eva was near.

The way she laughed and smiled throughout her immortal life was a thing of beauty, and I hated being the one responsible for dampening that light.

"Shh, I'll return one day," she whispered to the little child. His face was wet with tears. "Just be good for your mama, all right?"

He wrapped his tiny arms around her neck, then kissed her cheek. "I love you."

The air filled with sadness; became drenched with such a hollow emptiness that I sucked in a breath.

Vampires weren't supposed to be so emotional.

Leave it to a child to bring out the worst of the human weaknesses in all of us. God forbid I ever felt such a thing.

"I love you, too, John." He was one of the children she'd saved. He kept to himself. I don't believe he survived—not many did.

Eva set the boy on his feet. He reached up and captured one of her dark curls between his fingers, then he dropped it, turned on his heel, and walked off.

"He's precious," she said aloud, already sensing my presence. "It was his birthday. I couldn't allow him to think I didn't care anymore."

I crossed my arms. "Eva, there will always be something. A birthday, a holiday... You must leave him for good."

"I want children." Eva hung her head as I approached her from behind. "I've always wanted children."

I could taste her desperation in the air as tension swirled between us. I'd known for a while that Eva felt strongly for me—the way I felt for her.

But a union between a Dark One and a vampire would do nothing but present us with hurt feelings when a bond failed to form. We could not mate with each other.

And children were impossible.

"I can't give you that," I whispered, setting my hand on her shoulder. She gripped my fingertips, and I shuddered from her warm touch.

Eva turned, her green eyes beautiful as they gazed up into my cold depths. "We could adopt."

I smiled at that. "Humans adopt. And you and I...will never be."

"Immortality." She wrapped her arms around my neck. I never allowed such liberties. "Not for the faint of heart, hmm, Cassius?"

"No." The temptation to kiss her was too strong to deny any longer. My mouth descended, fusing with hers, creating a hum of energy between us as her blood heated, getting out of control. My touch cooled her as fangs descended past her top lip.

Our tongues twisted in a fight for dominance as I lifted her into my arms. The last thing we needed was to be seen in a forbidden embrace. Not only was she a Council member, but she was also a vampire—not mine.

She would end up with a snotty-nosed human.

One who would get her pregnant.

One who would love her like I never could.

Slowly, I pulled away from her, my hands pressing against her wrists as I lowered her arms to her sides.

"One day..." Her voice was filled with sadness. "I'll be mated to someone, and you'll forget all about me."

"I highly doubt I'll ever forget your taste, Eva."

A thick, flowery scent charged the air. Eva's eyes widened just as a voice said from behind me, "What have you done?"

Slowly, I turned.

Sariel's eyes were white, his hair a blazing rainbow of blue and black streaks. His feathers protruded, then shuddered as if tasting the wrongness in the air. "Survivors?"

He shoved past Eva and me and then pressed his fingertips to the door of the house.

"Two survivors. How many more? And why weren't they destroyed?"

I couldn't lie.

It wasn't in my makeup as a Dark One to want to lie to my creator—my father.

"I saved them," I admitted, grabbing Eva and shoving her behind me. "I saved twelve."

"Twelve!" Sariel roared, and the ground shook beneath our feet. "You were to destroy them all. Every. Last. One."

"I did not."

Sariel's wings turned purple, the color of angelic royalty. He was about to pass judgment. "Then you will die. Blood must always be spilled. You know this."

I nodded, unable to conjure any guilt for doing something that gave Eva happiness, no matter how temporary.

I took a step forward.

"No!" Eva shouted. "It was me."

"Eva!" I hissed out her name and shoved her body into the nearest wall. She stumbled back and glared. "Stay out of this."

"You will not die because of me." Her eyes glowed green, and her fangs elongated past her bottom lip. Her gaze snapped to Sariel. "If you want a life. Take mine. I asked Cassius to save them. It is I who is at fault."

"Very well." Sariel nodded.

"You cannot be serious." I charged Sariel, fists clenched. "She's a Council member. She's been around for centuries. You cannot simply eliminate her for one bad choice."

"Oh?" Sariel's head tilted to the side as he pulled a purple feather from his wing and held it out in front of him. The edge was black—the color of the Angel of Death. He meant to truly kill her. To make her no more. "We live by the rules, we die by the rules, Cassius. She broke the rules. She dies."

"But—"

Her head held high, Eva pushed past me and got down on her knees, her head bowed toward Sariel.

"Sariel, think about this." I knew reasoning with him would do nothing, but I couldn't stop myself. This was Eva. My Eva. I'd had her by my side since my creation. She was the reason the darkness wasn't so dark. Why I was always pulled back into the light. Without her, what was I?

"And there it is…" Sariel nodded. "She makes you weak. She makes you second-guess your decisions. Not that it matters. One of you must die for this serious lapse in judgment, and Eva is right. The fault lies with her. And I need you to lead the immortals. Therefore…" He held out the feather to me. "A life is taken."

"Cassius," Eva whispered, tears filling her eyes. "I love you."

Sariel sucked in a breath.

Now, he knew.

I'd failed him twice.

Because I loved her back.

"Eva, I will always love you," I whispered, taking the feather from Sariel and holding it over her head.

Sariel's anger was tangible. "Cassius, you are their king. She pays for your sin…kill her."

"I can't." My body was empty, *so* empty.

Eva locked eyes with me. "Cassius, promise me you'll check in on John. Promise."

At death's grasp, and still she worried about the boy.

I didn't understand that type of love. Maybe I'd never really loved, her after all. Had I?

"I promise." My voice shook as I pressed the tip of the feather to the base of her neck. It slid through her skin, and she slumped against my arms as immortality left her body.

Right before my very eyes, my dear friend, my love, aged. She aged so horribly her tight skin became wrinkled and paper-thin. It lost all the glow of youth, and her hair turned ten different shades of gray before finally falling out of her head. The bones in her body were brittle, the muscles detaching from their correct positions. And as she took her last breath, I saw what it would be like to be human, to love a human and watch them die.

The pain was unimaginable.

Her frail hand reached up and caressed my face with the lightest of touches. "Cassius…you will always be more light than dark."

She died.

In my arms.

"For her sacrifice," Sariel whispered, "the twelve children will live."

I didn't see Sariel again for five hundred years.

Later, when I finally did, I was already too far gone. I'd lost the mother of humanity.

I'd lost her.

And I'd set loose a monster, all because I loved her, and she'd asked—nay, begged—me.

I'd also cursed someone I knew I would most likely meet in my future, a person who would not survive it, at least according to my visions, weak as they were.

"But they won't." I shook my head and looked up at Sariel, the Archangel who'd birthed me by sleeping with a human, thus creating me as a Dark One—both Fallen and angelic. "Most will die before they reach sixteen. If they survive it, if they find each other, if I'm powerful enough to see it, then what? Do I kill them both?"

Sariel pulled a golden apple from his back and held it out in front of me. "Some futures are predestined. But, Cassius, we always have a choice. Take a bite."

"No." I hated him in that moment. "I won't ever truly fall."

"Says one who, by his choices, has already Fallen," Sariel said sadly. "You're the King of the Immortals. You roam the Earth with mixes of humanity from your mother in your blood. You question things, yet you want to rejoin the stars. What do you think happens when the first created is unleashed on this world? And what do you think happens when she finds a perfect match? What happens to the remaining gods who are allowed to roam? Chaos. Discord. Destruction. That will forever be on your head if you do not fix this. Maybe if they are raised with strong people, have principles, they will choose not to fall when the time comes... but to rise."

"I'll do it."

"Then..." He hid the apple. "You have made your first choice since falling. You will fix what Eva did by any means necessary, and you'll start with the immortal werewolf, who should not even exist. He should not have that blood running through his body or the gifts he does. You will start there, and you'll promise to forget you ever knew him. By all costs."

"And the girl?"

Sariel's nostrils flared. "Leave her to me."

Chapter Eight

Tarek

Present Day

"Well, this is great, just great." It's been an hour since Danu visited, and while Lilith is doing a stellar job of avoiding the need she has to both have sex with me and drink me dry, I don't really have high hopes. "So, can you at least tell me your story before you murder me?"

"No," she whispers, hanging her head in her hands. "You probably know all the gory details anyway. I'm one of the goddesses she controls to keep Discord,"—she uses air quotes—"from being released again. Balance has to remain the same. One slip of the scale to the wrong side, and disaster strikes. I'm sure Anubis knows all about it."

I'm instantly annoyed. "Disaster always teeters toward us, every second of every day. Why is now different?"

She smiles down at her hands. "You don't know your origins, do you?"

"Well, I clearly don't have a really attractive werewolf to feed off of and gain power from, so I can remember. All I know is that I came to live in Scotland when I was around eight. Everything before that is somewhat of a blur, a nice dream, maybe a nightmare. There was fire, darkness, and a small girl. And then Mason, my brother. That's all I remember. Maybe that's for a reason."

She nods as if she understands. How could anyone possibly? "Maybe it's best that way before you die—to not remember the things you should."

"I mean…" I try to laugh it off. "I'd like to at least remember all the sex we're going to have, but I'm leaning more toward I'll enjoy it in the moment, then go night night."

She smiles. It's so pretty, I really do want to lean in. But I wait for her to make the move first.

I'm no hero.

Maybe this is why I never saw my end. Ha, laughable that my end would come at the hands of the woman who started it all.

Lilith.

I should have done better math on that one and figured it out, but all I saw were her injuries, and all I felt was the need to save. I should have known someone that pretty, who fed off an immortal, was bad news.

Being saved isn't something to take lightly. I was saved as a child. Protected. And I swore I would always do the same, no matter what.

I wonder what Mason will do without me?

Timber, Cassius, Alex, Stephanie, Genesis...Horus, so many family members. And now this is how I go.

I sit up as best I can while being chained. The crazy goddess is gone but probably not too far away since she's extremely eager to get some blood in her.

"Let me guess..." I clear my throat. "Something about my blood mixed with what's inside you will give her a supercharge, and the more she does it over the years, the more powerful she gets. The more she's able to break her curse of having to look after the Fallen Goddesses—aka you—and the closer she gets to taking over all the divine power the Creator so generously stripped from her to limit her control of Their Creation... Am I close?"

"You're practically on fire." She folds her hands.

"And have you ever resisted?" I ask.

Slowly, she shakes her head. "No. I don't remember ever saying no to temptation, not in the last thousands of years. It is, after all, what I'm known for."

"And I think my life is hard sometimes." I try to smile, but it falls flat. I never really had to face my death, never really even thought about it. "Will I at least orgasm? Because if I get no orgasm, I feel like that's a no on this deal."

She actually laughs and covers her mouth with her hand. "Don't be funny right now. This sucks."

"Me thinks you do all the sucking."

"Me thinks you do all the moaning," she snaps right back. Our eyes meet, and I understand why she never says no. Because I don't want to say no either.

I want to say *yes* a million times. I want to consume her. I'm so hard from looking at her, I don't understand what's going on with my own body.

Her eyes swirl with gold around her pupils.

She leans down, then jerks back the minute I strain toward her, my mouth so eager for hers that it's all-consuming.

I have no choice but to allow it to happen, and she has no choice but to do it. This is the part of the story where the hero normally explains to the villain that everyone always has a choice, but I don't really see a way out of this. And because of my weakened state, all I can do is watch as she leans over my body with red eyes.

"Remember," I point out, straining toward her scent. God, it smells good. Like fresh rain and apples—like the earth. Like the Garden itself. "Orgasm or no deal."

She leans down and licks my neck, her tongue searing hot before she whispers in my ear.

"I was prideful to think I could ever resist you."

"I was prideful to assume I would want you to," I say honestly, body shuddering under her touch. She jumps on me and then straddles me. In one instant, she jerks my jeans completely down my body, moving so she can pull them off, all before straddling me again. I wince at the glorious pain of need, the wanting.

"Do it now. Do it," I whisper. I can't see straight, but I can feel. Hell, I can feel everything down to my core. My fangs elongate, my body telling me I want to mark her with my blood and scent, too. Maybe she'd enjoy the werewolf bite. But we typically don't just go around biting people who aren't our mates, just in case we accidentally make a mistake and claim out of lust.

I will claim her before I die.

Then again, it's like she's claiming me—she *is* claiming me.

She bites down on my neck. I let out a roar, my body bucking under hers. "Lilith!"

"Yours." She pulls back. My blood drips down her chin before she kisses me. I taste myself on her, I also taste *her* and lose control as my hips jerk. She's not giving me what I want. And it might kill me.

Lilith shakes her head and pulls back as if she's trying to regain some semblance of control. "If you keep moving, this will be over."

"If I don't, I might die," I say through clenched teeth. "Grab me."

Her eyes glaze over and turn so dark red they're nearly black. "Tarek—"

"Take what you need." I'm sweating now. "And give me what I'm owed for being tied to a fucking bed, getting fucked to death. At least give me—"

She reaches for my cock and squeezes. "This? Is this what you need?"

"More." I bite down on my lip, tasting my own blood. "More!"

She leans back and releases me with a scream before jumping off me and jerking off every inch of clothing she still has on, tossing them to the floor. She gets back on top of me and, without any warning whatsoever…

We're joined.

Mating.

One.

She moves against me so painfully slow that when I meet her thrust for thrust, it's all I can do to continue slowly. I didn't know you could be tortured this way.

"I need to be deeper." My voice is already going hoarse.

A low chuckle slips past her lips as she moves over me. "Silly werewolf, did you think it would only be one time?"

She slams her mouth back down on mine, and our tongues tangle, fighting for dominance. I'm so used to having that, but she owns me. She uses me in a way I welcome being used.

Fangs clash, and blood mixes on skin as she grips my biceps for leverage and pushes her body so hard onto mine that I get exactly what I ask for.

A scream bursts past her lips as she takes more blood, and then I see it. I see it all: the beginning of the Earth, her running through the Garden with a man by her side. I see her need to be free of the restraints of being the first, and her thirst as she walks up to the forbidden and stares.

"Why not us?"

"We don't ask those questions," he said, reaching for her hand. "We have our purpose, just like the trees, like the apples. We have our will. But we do not ask what we should not know, Lilith. Come."

He pulled her back against another tree and started kissing her, but the minute she tried to take control, he wouldn't allow it. He wanted to cater to her, serve her, but I felt her thoughts.

What about what I want? What about me catering to you? Why can we not be equals? Why are we created differently?

"I hear your thoughts." He shook his head. "They are not necessary."

Rage filled her. She didn't understand what it was until it was too late. Until she walked away from him and hid in the shadows. Then she looked up and said, "I think you made me wrong."

A whisper descended from the air. "I made you right, and you always have a choice in whether you stay or go. Know I will never keep you where you do not want to be. I love my Creations too much."

A tear slid down her cheek. "I'm broken. I want things I should not want."

"So, you will leave him? The first of them? You will leave perfection because you want?" the voice asked.

"What other choice do I really have?" She sighed and stood. "I'm not good enough for this. I question too much." She walked over to the tree, grabbed an apple, and took a bite. It was gold and massive. And then she saw too much.

"They forbade it." A man walked up to her. He was in golden armor and had a sword in his hand, ready to strike. "Take it with you. Take your curse and roam the Earth created so freely for you. When the time comes, you'll be given a choice again. This time, I hope it isn't a curse you choose...but life. And a future.

"Two days every year, you'll awaken. The rest of the time, you'll think things are normal. I see Discord in you, Lilith. And because you are the first to choose, you owe what is due and must pay for it in blood."

He sliced a symbol into her skin with his fingernail. "Now. Walk."

Panting, I look up at her. I'm still stuck in a sex-starved fever dream as she moves wildly over me, the pain of no release hitting me deeply, down to the bone.

"I saw—"

"Ignore that," she rasps and digs her fingernails into my chest. "And serve me."

So, I do.

I ignore it all.

And I fully give in to the feeling of being inside her, of truly knowing her. And in that moment...my future is even more clear.

It's her.

My mate.

And I will die before I ever get to claim her.

I scream as my release hits, over and over again. She jumps off me, high off immortal blood, then comes back, chest heaving. Her breasts are so perfect I jerk against the handcuffs, but I'm too weak and about to get weaker.

She climbs back onto me again and lowers herself. "Now, I'll take you rougher."

My eyes roll to the back of my head as I stupidly think to myself, *so much for a break for round two.*

The rest of the day flies by in a flash.

I lose track of how many times she says, "again." I'm bleeding everywhere, but all I can think is, *wow, she's really pretty.*

Chapter Nine

Cassius

I hated the thoughts that haunted me, the memories.

"Any word?" My wife, Stephanie, wraps her arms around me and pulls me close. She's no longer afraid of the sharp edges of my wings if they come out—she's powerful in her own right—and it's nice to be held.

I look down at my hands. "Do you ever blame me?"

Her dark hair swirls down by her waist as she lays me back against the bed and caresses my face, her blue eyes nearly twinkling like the stars. "Blame you for what?"

"Protecting you." I swallow. "For being what I am—?"

"Ninety-nine percent Archangel and one percent Dark One?" She winks. "Your father, Sariel, sacrificed everything for you. So much that he gave you his essence, so you'd one day go back to where you were always meant to be."

I snort out a laugh. "Heaven? Who, in all of this world, deserves that privilege?"

"Nobody," Stephanie says quickly. "But that's the point. We help the humans learn how to ascend and how to become their best selves, and then we hope that when Anubis and the Creator judge, they can become what they were born to be before…" She starts to choke up. "Before the Fall in Eden."

"The war in Greece, so much war."

"And…" She's quiet for a minute. "The day in Pompeii, when you were forced to make a choice and almost lost everything because of it. Do you ever wonder where they are?"

I smile. "I'd like to think I'm all-knowing, but I only see so many possibilities. I don't know the choices."

"But you see their faces." She rests her head against my chest. "Can you trust me and honor me with the answer of the face you see now? The grown child?"

My chest is tight.

I saw it tonight.

I saw it clear as day.

I saw him chained to the bed.

And then I saw *her*. The cursed goddess, Lilith, and Danu, who has the power to destroy it all if she can continue acquiring more blood for the next few years.

Lilith will suck him dry.

Then she'll relinquish the power of the blood because she has no choice.

And Tarek will die.

"I can't save him," I whisper to Stephanie. "It's free will. He is there of his own volition, whether he knows it or not."

"What do you mean?" She sits up. "Who?"

"He doesn't realize it yet," I say and start running my hands through her hair. "But he met his end the minute he met the beginning." I can barely get the words out. "The minute he met Lilith."

"The demon?" Stephanie frowns.

I shake my head. "She acts as a succubus as her punishment for the very thing she was created for—to be the mother of all. She's both Eris and Lilith. She's the one." I have to say her name. I *have* to say it. "She's one of the children Eva saved, who were reincarnated after her cursed beginning. She's the first…"

Stephanie's face pales. "Are you saying the Lilith you met is actually the first woman to be—"

I nod. I don't need her to say it.

"And Eva, as in Adam and Eve, is the one who saved a cursed child she knew had Discord forever in her soul?"

I nod again.

"Then what was your punishment?" Stephanie grips my hand tightly.

I smile and cup her face. "It was the last straw before the angelic part of me fell… Because I saved what should have died. I saved the beginning, when there was supposed to be an end. And I didn't just save her." I swallow slowly. "I saved several, though most are dead. I've secretly searched for the others, and we placed one in a very well-known family because of his powers."

Stephanie jerks back. "Are you talking about Tarek?"

"He's a werewolf. Had no idea when he was younger. Mason was there, and it just made sense. But he had something extra…" I squeeze my eyes shut. Never have I felt so much guilt. "He was one of the children during the destruction of Pompeii after the king mixed demon and angel blood to save his daughter—Tarek accidentally ingested both."

Stephanie drops my hand and looks away. "These are the details I need to know. So, where is he now? He's our family. We can't just abandon him."

"Stephanie." I pull her back against me. "I'm powerful. So are you, Alex, Timber… We all have the power to save, but at the end of the day, us saving him isn't really saving him. The point of free will is that you sometimes have to save yourself in order to become what you were born to be. So now, we wait."

"Will he die?" she asks seconds later.

I don't admit the fear, so I merely answer her. "Fear is not welcome here." Then I wave my hand over her face and snap my fingers. "Sleep."

I know it's wrong to use my power on her, but she's pregnant, exhausted, and she'll worry.

Yet again, I suddenly miss my father, his wisdom, the way he looked at things. I cannot imagine walking through life, seeing all the choices people can make, and watching them make the wrong ones over and over again.

But now I know.

Because the minute Tarek started working at that bar, and the minute the girl he held hands with so many years ago saw him…

His fate was sealed. And so was hers.

I grab one of my purple feathers and flick it into the air. "I hope you know what you're doing, Creator."

It was silent for several minutes before a childlike voice whispered. "I always do."

Chapter Ten

Tarek

It was a fever dream. I was hot, sweaty, exhausted, and sticky with blood, and she was on me, breathing heavily, sighing against my chest.

Maybe by way of sex, this was always my journey.

Death by sex.

Wow, the things they could have taught me in elementary school. Ha. I'm delirious. I know I don't have much time left. My eyes roll to the back of my head as I pass out into more dreams, ones I hate, yet ones I feel I need to see before I go.

Ones of my past.

Reminding me I have no future.

"Eva!" Cassius's voice was thick with emotion as he held nothing but dust in his hands. Like diamonds, the glittery particles spread in a perfect circle around his body. His head was hung, his shoulders tense.

Sariel stood behind him, looking just as menacing as ever. Then he disappeared, leaving Cassius alone.

I'd never seen a Dark One cry. Didn't know they were capable of it. Ever since my birth, I'd had trouble even conjuring up watery eyes. Although I felt sadness, I couldn't express it.

The voice in my head narrating the vision was male, familiar. Was it Alex? Someone else? Them? Was it someone else, or was I really just so delirious I was making things up?

Cassius was wrapped in a type of red toga, a sword at his side. He slowly pulled it from its silver casing and held it out in front of him.

I could feel pain all over me just hearing the voice narrate—like nails running down a chalkboard over and over again.

"Don't." Ethan appeared in front of Cassius. "Put the sword down, brother."

"She's gone," Cassius whispered. "I have nothing left."

"You have Alex," Ethan joked. "He's like a two-year-old. He needs guidance.

You know how new he is."

Cassius continued to stare at the long sword. "I want to forget the pain."

"You'll go dark if you do, Cassius. You know this. Forgetting emotions isn't human."

"I'm not human!" Cassius spat. "I'm an angel!" He stood to his full height, his body shimmering with iridescent white and purple hues as he called upon his angel blood, pushing the humanity so far away that it hurt my eyes to look at him. Snow fell in the spot over his head. "I am to be worshipped!"

"Brother..." Ethan's voice was still calm. "You are Fallen."

As if a reminder of what he would never be, wings appeared at Cassius's sides, but they were completely black.

And dripping with blood.

As the storm increased, what had once been bright turned so dark I stumbled backward.

Cassius's eyes went black, too, his teeth elongating into fangs before his body grew another foot.

"Evil and good always did have a problem coexisting," Ethan said in a bored tone. "Come back, brother...killing yourself is not the answer, for you will lose your soul and become your greatest nightmare. Meaning one of us will eventually have to kill you, and I've hunted enough friends. Don't make me hunt my family."

Cassius fell to his knees, the diamonds of dust bursting into the air. He lifted his hand and caught a few particles, pressing them to his heart. "So I never forget the pain of remembering."

"Pain," Ethan answered just as Mason appeared, sword raised, "isn't reserved for mere humans. It's for everything in Creation. It would not be fair if we never experienced it."

"I don't want to feel." Cassius stood, sheathing his sword and facing both men. "I refuse it."

Mason looked unsure of what to say, but Ethan nodded. "One day, you will regret that choice. And I do hope I'm still alive to see it."

I jerk awake.

How many hours have gone by? And why did Cassius kill the one he loved? I knew he had a tragic past, but why would he become Fallen? I can't even rub my blurry eyes; all I can do is exist with a beautiful woman destined to kill me on my chest and the need for food.

"So, you saw?" she asks, not opening her eyes but clinging to me tighter. "You'll see more and more as you die. It will get stronger as your body weakens. You'll see what I know, and you'll see what the universe knows, but it won't do any good, Tarek. I wish that knowledge gave you power right now, but the only person with power is me. And then her."

I snort out a laugh. "Well, can I at least ask the girl who just screwed me what her opinion is on all of this? You know, why you want me, why she wants me? I'm not a god, I'm a werewolf. So, best-case scenario, you have to shave more once I die."

I feel her smile against my chest before she leans up onto her arms to stare down at me. "I don't want you to die. I want to save you."

"That feels very sexually exploitative to me. No offense."

Her smile spreads wide. Her short blue hair is even beautiful while sticking to her cheeks with sweat. "Maybe you'll be reincarnated and marry someone wonderful. Someone who can give you the life you deserve."

I find it hard to swallow as I try to say something or think of an answer to give her, but all I have is the one passed down to me by Mason that day—when he and I were abandoned.

"Some immortals are reborn for specific things—but you're different, Tarek. I'm sorry I can't watch you grow, but I know you'll do a good job here." He looked around the underground tunnels, part of our Scottish castle. "We can't explain some destinies, and when I brought you here, I already knew that yours would be different."

"You make it sound like I'm cursed."

"No. Not you specifically." He looked down at his hands and rubbed them together. "Just know that some destinies are fulfilled by darkness, and others by light."

"And mine?"

He gripped my shoulder with his hand and squeezed. "Only the Creator knows."

"And my gifts?" I asked.

"No need to keep them a secret. They're gifts, after all. But sometimes, the very thing you think is a gift is a curse."

"Why?"

"Because..." Mason pulled away from me and stood to his full height. "Because you won't see it coming. You won't see anything about your destiny but will forever watch others live out theirs. If you ask me, that's not a blessing."

Darkness washed over me. "Do you know who my real parents are?"

Mason shook his head slowly. "Nobody does, but I imagine they were very powerful at one point. You don't have the sight because your mom was a werewolf. It's because your father was considered a human god. But all I know are the rumors. You were one of the twelve children saved and are one of the remaining three. You were kept alive for a purpose, but I cannot lie to you. Sometimes, a purpose means your end."

I stood and reached for him, pulling him in for a hug as I said, "So be it."

Chapter Eleven

Lilith

His unique power slithers through my blood. I feel him in every pulse: his memories, life, friendships, family.

A tear runs down my cheek.

He'll miss them.

And now, because his blood is inside me, I will, too. I'll miss them all so much. And I'll miss the fact that I knew at one point who to thank for saving my life.

"Stories." I rub his back. "Are sometimes like nightmares, Tarek."

His breathing is heavy, his hand weak as he reaches for me. "I have those, too. The nightmares. I see fire and brimstone. I should have asked Timber if that's the Underworld, but I vaguely remember a girl. I held her hand. She clutched mine back. And what nightmare includes holding a pretty girl's hand in Hell?" He deliriously chuckles. "So hot. Ice cream would have been nice."

"Did it even exist back then?"

"Hmm?" He growls, his nails starting to grow as they dig into my skin—his instinct to fight when he knows he'll die soon. "Sorry." He retracts them instantly. "My thoughts aren't alive right now."

"You mean cohesive?"

"Mm-hmm, that." I can feel his yawn and look up into his eyes, but they're closed, and I know that's how they'll stay.

I don't know how long we have, but I assume it's not long before Danu walks in to a corpse, then steals the very blood she needs me to take to gain more power and freedom.

Will it happen a dozen more times?

A hundred?

I don't know the answer, but I do know she's getting more and more powerful. And at some point, she needs to be stopped.

Free will.

Good and evil coexisting.

What absolute tragic bullshit.

I can't bear it.

I can't look at Tarek without wanting to cry. Why him? Why did it have to be the very first immortal to save me other than the Council? Why did it have to be someone whose thoughts were so pure it hurt? Why did it have to be a prince of the Earth and someone who will never know how truly special he actually is?

"Eyes," I whisper.

He blinks at me a few times. "What?"

"Give me your eyes."

He smirks. "Be more specific. Do you like physically need them, or do you want me to look at you? Because right now, I see a dozen of you. I'm delirious as hell."

"You're going to die," I say as plainly as possible.

He sighs. "Yes, thank you for the reminder. This is a really inspirational speech. Please, go on. Don't hesitate to detail every horrible moment."

I cup his face with shaking hands and hold tight. "But before you do, you need to know."

"Know what? I swear, if Alex did this all as a prank…" We both know he's just being sarcastic, but I smell no fear on him, only acceptance. Which makes it so much harder to do what I need to do.

I lightly dig my fingers into his temples. "You know I'm the first, and the first was blessed with the power to see things. But because of the wars I caused, because I did not do what I was created for, I was cursed to be guided by the rest of the goddesses. Eris didn't like it and got into trouble, so was basically linked to me—to constantly be imprisoned to whatever power I get from immortals. Every year, for two days, I feed. And when I do, I go for the most powerful source to seduce, only to wait until it's time for her to wake me up again. Pitiful existence. And I only gain memories when I drink from that source. But I also gain *theirs*. And yours were not what I expected. So, before I kill you, do you want to know?"

I sense his hesitation as his head lolls to the side. "What if it's depressing? I really don't want to be depressed before I die. Hey, speaking of, you should show me more boob. I can't even touch you. I should at least get to see, right?"

My smile is sad. It's painful, it feels horrific, and yet I share it with him because he needs something good to look at before the end.

"I don't know…am I part badass?" He chuckles and strains against the handcuffs again. "Maybe I have blood from a poet in me. Maybe I'm part demon. Maybe I'm just like you."

"No." My eyes burn as I see flashes of Pompeii, holding hands with other children being saved. The ash hurts as memories go in reverse to one of the angels at the banquet.

The angel who said he wanted to help feed the humans.

"He asked for sacrifices." I could barely keep my tone even as I saw the vision of a man in all black walking slowly through the banquet hall, encouraging the orgy already taking place. His smile was cruel. Cassius was there, trying to stop him—no, he'd been sent to stop him.

I bite into my wrist and hold it to Tarek's lips. "Drink and watch."

He opens his mouth, the rich mixture of his blood—like the rawness of the Earth—mixes with the pureness of mine.

One who was first created.

Tarek's eyes go black like mine as the first drop of our mixed blood falls onto his tongue. He doesn't need much. Black eyes widen, and then I'm synced with him.

The Fallen Archangel continued to walk down the banquet hall, his hood heavy over his head, his smile still cruel and all-knowing.

I didn't like it.

I didn't like any of it, but I could feel myself holding someone's hand. When I looked over, I saw a small boy close to my age.

"Are you afraid?" I asked.

He had beautiful, honey-brown hair and dark eyes. "No." He shrugged. "I don't remember anything really after…after." He frowned. "Did they do something to us?"

I nodded. "Yes. Him." I didn't point at the dark angel; I just watched him walk until he finally stilled amid the chaos of the party. Slowly, he turned his head and made eye contact with us, freezing us both in place.

"He's coming." I gulped. "He's going to do it again."

It felt like an eternity until he stood in front of us and then went to his knees, still towering over our small bodies. "Beautiful." He pulled back his hood. "I never knew you would both turn out so perfect being reborn this way. But it looks…" He tilted my head, then Tarek's. "It looks like the perfect combination of angelic blood and that of the firsts…"

His white eyes narrowed into tiny slits. "Though we can't always plan for some things. Can we, Lilith?" He stopped examining us and turned to Tarek. "And others are better than expected. My, my, the age you have in your blood. The wisdom you have in your mind. They'd be smart to keep you hidden from us, for I would feed from you for centuries."

He laughed. "If I debased myself enough to do so. But still, I'm not fully Fallen yet. I just want you to understand that the Creator doesn't care. They never did… The stars will fall from the sky because they choose to save immortals and humanity. They choose to fall because that is their purpose given by the Creator. Want to guess yours?"

I started shaking so hard my teeth chattered. Tarek pulled me closer against him.

It's like I'm inside my small body again, like I'm back in that moment when I thought all would be lost.

"You." He pointed at me. "Were here in the beginning. You hold the soul of Lilith, the first before Eve—or Eva as some say. And you…" He turned his head to the side. "Are the son of Enoch. Some might say you house one of the only human souls in eternity that never died. Makes you wonder how I was able to do it."

He leaned in and whispered, "Because, dear child, I was the angel who killed him. I ripped him to shreds in Heaven and then fled, taking that tiny blue remnant of a soul with me and then gifting it to you. You should say thank you."

"You're bad," Tarek said boldly. "And you will be punished."

Danu walked up behind the angel and laughed. "Playing with children, Phanuel, when you could be playing with me? A goddess?"

Phanuel stood to his full height, his jet-black hair falling down his back. "It's good that we both like games. Shall we start a new one?"

Danu clapped her hands. "Yes, yes, yes! I've been so bored."

Her white hair bounced around her waist as she clung to Phanuel and wrapped her arms around him, crushing his black tunic.

"A bet, then." Phanuel's grin was evil. "I'm going to give them my blood. I'll gift her to you as punishment for what she possesses and what caused part of the Fall and cursed us all… And I'll give him a living Hell. What he thinks is his blessing will become his curse and what will end up killing him. The gift he has, the blood he carries, they will be his end. And she will be the one to bring it. After all, she holds the apple in her soul. The minute you're powerful enough to extract it…"

He turned to Danu. "You'll be able to control her, only allow her to exist for a certain period of time every year. The same with the rest of the goddesses. I wonder who will die first. Who will survive? So, yes, let's take some bets. Will she"—he pointed at me—"last because of her origin? Or will she constantly create Discord? Ah!" He snapped his fingers. "What an incredible future you will have."

He turned to Tarek. "And you, my child. What an incredible end."

Danu laughed. "We have our own little Adam and Eve. The Fall will be massive, the blood powerful."

"Why else would I use children and bring down the souls from the Creator? I want power. But what I really want…" He looked around. "Is to be entertained before I die. I can't wait to—"

A sword suddenly went through his chest, dripping golden blood onto the ground in slow, purposeful drops. Danu moved around and licked the tip of the blade, then moved again and thrust it deeper from behind. "You may be a nearly Fallen Angel, but you were so easy to manipulate, screw, and feed lie after lie. Do you want to know why I caught you unawares?"

His head lolled as she leaned in and whispered in his ear. "Because you wanted. And whenever we want, we lust and tend to forget everything around us. Truly, though. Thank you for this delicious blood. You were one of the best in Heaven before you believed my lies. Now, I'll send you to Hell and use every drop of your blood." She turned to Tarek. "On him."

A sudden explosion happened in the distance. There was so much ash and smoke. Within seconds, I saw Tarek lying on the ground, gold blood pooling in his mouth.

I rushed over and held him up, but it was too late.

He'd already swallowed.

He had been immortal to begin with. Now? Now, he was…other.

Now he's an abomination with powers only the Heavens can understand. Now, he will forever be in isolation, lost but not understanding why, even with power and a family. He will never love.

Chapter Twelve

Cassius

Ethan slams his hand against the table, nearly slicing it in half. "We have to do something."

"No," Horus answers before I can. "Trust me, I want to save Tarek, too, but even if we knew where they were taken, we can't force our will on them—"

"Quite honestly,"—Timber grabs his mug of coffee and sits down on the counter—"if I hear one more time that you can't force will onto people, I'm going to lose my mind. Can you force people to make choices? Oh, I don't know…" he says mysteriously with a smirk that I'm not entirely comfortable with. "I mean, we can. There are just… consequences."

Stephanie leans in. "What kind?"

He shrugs. "Well, in the Underworld, you need balance, same as up here." He taps the table with his fingers. "In the old days, you had to bring in your gold to earn acceptance. We did away with that, and because Horus can more or less see souls or pull them from bodies the same as I can, we started to just check if they were pure."

"So many were not," Horus says and takes a sip of coffee. "Oh, sorry, my thoughts are all over the place. But we can't save them because, apparently, the Earth still functions the same as it did before, just twisting on its axis and giving everyone air. I mean, until it resets again. Which…that shit gets rough."

"Resets," we all say in unison.

Timber sighs and leans back, coffee still in hand—a red cup that says *Bite me*, which would be amusing if I wasn't so worried about Tarek and Lilith.

"Okay." Timber stands. "I can check if they're in the Underworld, but other than that…" He looks over at me, his jaw clenched. "They're on their own. And my fear is…"

He doesn't finish his sentence.

I squeeze my eyes shut.

"Creator," I whisper. "Please, hear my cry. Hear me now. A friend—a family member—is in danger, and I don't know what caused it. But we need…" I pause. "We need the stars. We need more power. I can save him, but I can't go outside the visions I see. Tarek's will is strong, but he can't see his future. He can't see anything…he's blind. He's probably being fed from, and I have no way to save him other than to pull a corpse from—"

"Stop," a voice commands.

I look around, but nothing appears.

The tone is robotic in nature.

"Let," it whispers.

The entire group looks around. We're powerful enough to kill most things, but this has no body. It has nothing. And in all my years of existing, I've never experienced the power coming from it.

"Let," it repeats. "Let him fulfill it."

I shake my head. "He's only a werewolf. He can't."

The voice sounds again. "Dear, sweet angel…he's so much more than he can possibly know. Older than you. Smarter." The voice chuckles. "No offense, sweet angel. Thank you for what you do. When the time is right, They'll let you know."

"Who are you?" I stand. I'm used to talking to the Heavens, I'm used to immortal creatures, but this is different.

Everything in the air feels hot and cold all at once. Sweat drips down my cheek and falls onto the table.

I raise my hands to freeze the room when a chuckle sounds again. "Oh, Cassius. What a great immortal you have become. I've watched for so long. After all, that's what we do. We watch." Chills run down my spine. "We watched then, and we watch now. If you need me, please use my name. I am Uriel, angel of repentance, guardian of Eden. They have the apple, but only Tarek can retrieve it and make things right. We do this for Lilith. We do it for humanity. We do it for the first. She's suffered too long. Her journey has also been long—to find him. So now, we need you to sit and prepare yourselves."

A chill runs down my spine again. "For?"

"Genesis."

Chapter Thirteen

Tarek

I'll kill her. I'll end her. The number of years I've survived on top of the soul I hold from being a son of Enoch, someone who walked with the Creator, someone who knew things he should have never known...

Someone who helped the Fallen Angels before they were sent to the Abyss.

I see it all. I see it clearly.

The Creator locked up the angels. They sent them to the corners of the Earth. And for the select few?

Chained in the Euphrates.

I look at Lilith. I watch her sleep, knowing I'll soon die, and she'll remember nothing. And then I wish.

I remember.

Stars.

They chose to fall.

The power of a star could save us—the power of a sacrifice. A tear runs down my cheek. I don't want to ask. I don't want to, but then I look at Lilith and know she's my destiny. I realize I can stop all of this with one wish, one whisper.

I'm no hero.

I'm a son of Enoch, I have his blood. I'm a werewolf prince. I walk this Earth, knowing I was put here for a purpose.

Maybe this is it.

Saving the first.

Saving Lilith.

I'm so weak, I can barely breathe. She lays across me, my blood all over her face, the look in her eyes unreadable.

"Tell me a story," I rasp.

Her head lolls to the side. "What's the point? I've found the one person I've been searching for since he held my hand in Pompeii, only to kill him. Seriously, what's the point? You'll die, and I won't remember this. Danu will take care of that."

"Then look at me." I use the last of my strength to reach for her face. "Kiss me goodbye. Make sure to bury me...well, I mean, if you remember."

"That's not funny."

"I'm not laughing. But you're really pretty. And don't worry, I don't need you to be my hero. I don't need a rescue. Sometimes, the best stories end in sacrifice."

A tear slides down her cheek, passing by her glorious blue hair that's sticking to the blood on her skin. It falls to my chest, and I whisper in my head, *worth it*. It was all worth it because I found the one who held my hand and stood by my side. The one that was there when angels fell, when we were taken advantage of, when the world was destroyed.

She never left me.

I might have Enoch's blood, I might be a werewolf, but nobody is coming to save us now—and they shouldn't.

But I can save her.

I can save her from this Hell.

I can make sure she wakes up tomorrow remembering everything. I can give her the gifts given to me. What I always thought were curses and isolation, over and over again. I can give the last of me to the first of Creation.

I can finally breathe.

It's like my soul knows it's time to flicker out.

It's like my body realizes that, in the end, maybe the best way to survive is to become the person who doesn't.

I smile up at her. "Thanks for the orgasms."

She shakes her head. "Again, not funny."

"I thought it was funny. You know, good story. I'm a werewolf prince."

"I know."

"And we control the Earth, we protect it, we have special powers. I mean, *I* do since I have the blood of Enoch and that creepy angel dude. But do you know what else?"

Tears keep streaming down her face. "What? What else?" She presses her lips to my neck and starts sobbing. "What else, Tarek? Tell me."

"We"—I look up at the dark ceiling—"can control the stars."

She jerks back. "Nobody ever told me that."

"You are Lilith." I cup her face with my shaking hands. "You've been cursed to roam for too long without any sort of rest. It's time, daughter of the Creator. It's time to go home."

"I have none."

My hand drops against my chest while the other covers her face. "Of course, you do. It's right here." My heartbeat is off, but the gesture is the same. I always wondered what death would look like for me. All I saw was darkness, but now I know why it was dark.

Because I had to search for the star.

I had to look for her light.

I hold both hands up to the ceiling, close my eyes, and whisper, "I need one to fall. Choose."

The room begins to shake as most of my strength leaves my body, and my essence pulses in mourning.

A bright light cracks through the ceiling and drops next to the bed, crashing into tiny little crystals. Then a beautiful woman with ebony skin and bright blue eyes walks toward us and kneels. "It is my honor to give you my light."

Danu runs into the room with a blade.

But all I focus on is the beauty of the star of the light that pours out of her. Her willingness to give of herself no matter the cost. I know that once they fall, the Creator has a special place for the stars. And she does, too.

There is no war. There is no division. There is only sacrifice, followed by honor, love, joy.

Peace.

The world could be healed by someone like her. And now the first will be.

The star smiles and reaches for my hand. "Blood must always be spilled. A sacrifice must always be made." She grabs Lilith's hand and squeezes it. "It has been an honor to watch you."

The blade Danu has goes directly into the star's back.

As the first drop of blood descends, I grab it and press it to Lilith's forehead.

My last deed.

My final sacrifice.

Everything goes dark as I hold the star's hand.

Everything goes black as Lilith is finally filled with light.

Purpose.

Chapter Fourteen

Cassius

The Earth trembles.

The table beneath us suddenly breaks in half.

All of us jerk away from it.

"Something's off." Mason looks around. "Something is…" He looks down at his hands. They have blood mixed with a weird crystalline substance on them.

I know exactly what it is.

"He…" I can barely breathe as my wife grabs my hand. "He sacrificed."

Timber collapses into his chair. "He called a star."

"He's gone." Horus's eyes blaze white. "He's no longer of this Earth. He's…" A tear runs down his cheek. "He fulfilled his purpose."

"No." Genesis, Ethan's wife, walks into the kitchen and slams her hands down on the table. She's been with her children and trying to make sure we remained fed. We attempt to keep everyone away from danger, but she's always been one to run into it. Maybe that's why she's one of my best friends.

"No," she repeats. "It's me."

"Huh?" Alex pipes up. "What's you?"

"The beginning." She starts to sob. "I was taking a nap with the kids and…" She starts shaking so hard I'm concerned I need to grab her or have Ethan pull her away from the situation. I stand. "Cassius, I swear, if you touch me or send me back upstairs, I will find a way to murder you."

I hold up my hands.

Ethan backs away.

All of us are silent as we watch her regain some semblance of calm.

"Lilith is the beginning. Eva saved her—aka Eve. The minute I heard that sound, I had a vision." She swallows and takes a deep breath as if regaining her composure. "It's been predestined. We have to go back, all of us. Our entire families and the Council. We need to go back. We have one more task, and it won't be pretty." She jerks her head toward Alex and Horus. "Can you still move through time?"

Horus sighs. "I can't. I used my one-way ticket."

Alex gulps and raises his hand. "Actually, mine was refundable." Nobody laughs, but Ethan and Mason moan out loud like he's the most annoying person in the world, which he is. "Okay, no jokes. Sorry, I thought we were Vikings. Anyway, since I have the blood of Ra…" Nobody says anything. "Wow, still no applause? Okay, right then. I can try, but that won't help our current situation."

I hang my head. "We should at least retrieve his body. We owe him that."

Mason's quiet.

All of us wait for someone to say something, but then he walks over to Genesis and grabs her by the shoulders. "You're the beginning. So was Lilith. Your name *means* beginning. Therefore, I'm going to ask you for a favor."

"Anything," Genesis says.

Ethan starts to move, but I grab him by the arm and hold him back. "Let her."

"She could die."

"We all could." I turn to him. "But as one of my oldest friends, I need you to listen. I need you to stay calm. We all need your help. We've fought wars. We've razed cities. We've protected humans for this long. Let this one do what we can't."

Ethan turns away from me, his green eyes blazing. "If I lose what I love, I lose it all."

"Losing"—I put a hand on his shoulder—"is part of life. No immortal can escape it. And even if you could, escaping pain is like ignoring what teaches us to stand back up and fight. Look at it differently. Losing us, all of us in this room, to save the world." My past comes back to haunt me. "You have to ask yourself, how many could you save? How many? One? Two? Three? How many is enough? If we all sacrifice ourselves, would it be worth it to save ten?"

"Yes," he chokes out.

"How about nine?"

"Yes." He starts crying silently next to me.

"Ethan, what if we sacrificed all to save one?"

He leans against my shoulder and looks up, green eyes clear. "Yes, Cassius. Yes."

"And that"—I nod—"is why we were put here as the Immortal Council. That is why we exist. Because if we can save just one, we have done the job given to us."

"Okay." His nostrils flare, and I know he's annoyed, upset, and frustrated with me. But the rest fall silent, watching our interaction, knowing I'm not wrong.

When my father gave me his power and sacrificed his ability to be an Archangel, when the Creator gave us all the gifts we have and created races within the world…

I realized it would come to this one day.

Will you sacrifice the few to save the many?

Will you sacrifice everything you know and love?

Will you fall on your own sword?

Humans tend to be selfish. Immortals are no different.

I walk toward Genesis and hold out my hand. "Show me what you saw and tell me how I can help."

Mason relaxes next to me and touches my shoulder. "How we can *all* help."

Genesis grips my hand tightly. "Watch, son of the Watchers." Her eyes blaze green before a vision appears.

I see blood.

Danu.

Lilith.

A star falling.

Tarek taking his last breath. "Wait." I gasp. "Wait."

I keep watching as Lilith reaches over to him and pours her blood into his mouth while the star dies and then Danu stabs her.

And then I see.

"Angels."

Chapter Fifteen

Lilith

"You're both idiots." Danu laughs and starts dragging me across the dirt. I see a body next to me that I assume is either the star or Tarek.

"Where are we?" I ask.

She rolls her eyes. "Where else? I'm going to feed on you, then feed you to the Fallen Angels in the Euphrates. They get quite hungry. Heard a rumor that even Medusa is down there, just sucking a Fallen Angel dry. Must be Hell for him, over and over again."

I can't move.

I'm strong but weak. By the looks of the blood on her lips, she's probably already fed. I feel half-dead and can't even save Tarek.

"What did you do with him?" I plead. "Is he okay?"

Danu laughs. "He's currently enjoying time on the dirt, looking up at the stupid star he called, probably wondering in his death if he did the right thing. But, spoiler alert, all that did was make it so you got superhyped on star blood, which in turn just gave me more power. Some people are just idiots, and you slept with one. I hope you make a better choice the next time I wake you up for two days. Because, wow."

It doesn't make sense. The star should have given me unlimited power for at least a few hours. Did she already drain it?

Frowning, I touch my forehead. Why is it wet?

Wait. Her blood.

My skin's hot to the touch. Danu isn't paying attention since she's busy dragging me through dirt and water.

I touch it again, and my fingertip burns.

My body is covered in dust and water as she tosses me toward the cave's dark entrance.

This is it.

We failed.

And she's going to survive again and again.

I have no knife.

I have no way of hurting her.

And my curse continues.

I press my hands against the earth and pause as rocks start shaking.

The power of the Earth. The power of a prince of the Earth. The star. I look up and grin. "Bet you weren't expecting this."

I slam my hands down so hard the earth beneath us begins to crack, causing an earthquake so loud and big that Danu starts screaming as it gives way beneath her feet.

"You'll free him!" she yells. "You'll free them both. Stop!"

I look up at her and grin, keeping my hands planted on the ground. "I heard he's the worst Fallen Angel of them all. I heard Medusa hates you. *And* I heard they have three more chained beneath this very soil. Try to survive the Ancients. I dare you." Rage burns in my soul. This is what she deserves. And if I'm ended, what better way to go than with the goddess who wields what should have never been hers to control?

Danu jumps on me. My body burns where she touches. She rips my hands from the dirt, rolling me over onto my back. Her eyes are black with fury, her weight so heavy across my chest that it's hard to breathe. I suck in a sharp breath. It really is the end. How tragic that I was the beginning, and now this is how my story reaches its completion—being killed by someone who, by all measures, should be weaker than me. "I will live forever. You are going to die right now. I'm putting you out of your misery. Isn't that what you wanted, dearest Lilith? I can feed off another being. I'll make it slow and painful. I mean, I wanted you every year, but now you've just become a nuisance. So, what are your last words?" Black claws extend from her fingertips toward my neck. "Before I slit your throat."

I smile as tears run down my dirty face—at least they're warm, at least I know how it all ends, right? Should I be thankful? I look up at the stars. They're so pretty. Creation always has taken after the Creator. I want to reach for them; instead, I just smile. "My last words? Sometimes, the world doesn't need a hero. It needs a sacrifice."

I look away from her and at the stars again. "Thank you...for choosing to fall for someone like me."

They shine.

And all I can think again is, *how pretty.*

How very pretty.

I open my mouth to say *"thank you"* when the earth trembles a second time. But I'm no longer touching it.

Footsteps slam loudly against the ground, shaking Danu right off me. Slowly, I get up while she screams.

It's the Council.

With all their wives by their sides.

Cassius is in front with Timber and Horus. They join hands as something gold flickers between what they touch. In an instant, they kneel.

Why are they suddenly kneeling?

Everyone lowers themselves behind them as if they weren't just trying to go to war.

"Uriel," Cassius calls out. "Danu has the apple. Send them down!"

The stars shine so brightly that it's hard to focus. When I look to my right, I see the golden apple—what started the Fall, the war—Danu has it in her hand.

I use all my strength to reach for it but can't quite get close enough. Then, another hand grabs it.

"Tarek!" I yell.

He looks like he just fought seven wars but snatches the apple out of her hands and then stumbles toward the cave.

"Tarek, no!"

"Yes." He falls to his knees. "What was once Fallen must be restored. The star said so in her last moments. We have to restore the Fallen, the beginning, you, the end."

He throws the apple into the dark cave.

And as he does, the stars light up above us to the point where I can't see anything anymore. But I *can* hear. I hear it all.

A rumbling so loud you'd think the world was ending.

Danu starts screaming, covering her ears. Maybe that's what happens when monsters meet their maker.

Then, all at once, what looks like ten thousand angels descend to the ground, all covered in full red armor. The sound is like rumbling thunder hitting the earth. Silence no longer exists.

There's only them.

I look to the right and watch as swords plunge into the ground. They're black and sharp and stay there, causing the earth to rumble even more—no, not rumble, it groans as they stand. Nobody moves. Nobody breathes. They're like statues waiting for something.

They look toward the cave as if expecting a miracle to occur, when I know, sadly, curses are more common. Yet I look along with them as Danu continues screaming in alarm like she can't handle what's going on around her. Is it the supernatural? Is it the fact that the swords went into the earth? I have no clue. I'm probably just as clueless as the goddess is at this point, and so delirious I think I'm seeing things.

For the first time, I realize that the rumors are true as Bannik and Medusa walk out into the stars beneath the moon, standing tall.

Medusa is gorgeous, her red and black hair falling in dreadlocks to her waist. Her eyes are closed.

Bannik grabs her hand, and I've never seen a man so tall.

He's truly a Fallen Angel, one of the first, not from the Garden but from being a Watcher. From becoming what he should have never been.

He locks eyes with me and then turns toward Horus. "Did you find my star?"

Horus walks forward, and it's like everything moves in slow motion. "I promised I'd make a star."

"That you did." Bannik's reddish-black hair is braided down his back. "And did you keep your promise?" A tear runs down his cheek.

Horus nods and looks at Timber, who looks at Cassius. They all walk forward. I have no idea what's going on, but Danu is suddenly paralyzed next to me, her eyes following the movement of everything.

I slowly get up and wait.

I really have no idea what's going on.

The angels wait, the army still with their swords in the soil. Then they shock the crap out of me and bow over their weapons.

"Ah," Cassius says. "This was a long time coming, Archangel." He kneels—the King of the Immortals on Earth, an Archangel in his own right, kneeling in front of Bannik, the worst of them all. He spreads his arms wide. "What better way to welcome you back than to bring you the stars?"

In a sudden motion, several fall to the Earth next to the angels. They stand and bow, and then...

They start to sing.

I don't know the language.

I don't know what's even happening.

"Welcome." Cassius stands. "Dear brother...you can hear them again."

Was it the apple that released him that he needed all this time? The very first Fallen?

Bannik jerks his head to me. "And you."

This can't be good.

He smiles. "Not you." He nods. "You're safe. But *you*…" He grabs Danu by the neck and throws her against the ground. "Taking advantage of something so pure, something so new. You were there with us in the beginning, but you know the best part?" Danu shrieks and flails as he leans down and whispers, "We know your end. We always have. Timing is, after all, everything."

It's over in seconds. He flicks his wrist, and the apple appears again. He slams it against her mouth, shoves it in tightly, and whispers. "Fall."

I expect something weird, but I *don't* expect the actual ground beneath her to disintegrate as she does, indeed, fall into a fiery pit, only to be covered up seconds later.

Bannik stands.

Cassius walks over to him, joined by Horus, and finally Timber. They watch the earth heal. Mason follows and stands behind them.

And Tarek?

He crawls.

He moves toward the immortals. "Thank you."

"Thank the stars." Bannik looks down. "Must I sacrifice myself again to save another immortal? When will my turmoil be done? Hmm?"

I know he sacrificed himself to save Horus earlier, but does he even possess enough power to do it again?

"No need." A female voice sounds as Medusa leans over Tarek. "Look at me."

"It's a curse!" I yell. "She'll turn you into stone."

Medusa's eyes are closed, but she turns in my direction. "My dear sister, it's only a curse if I make it so. Now, open your eyes, Tarek. Let me give you what you need."

Tarek pants on the ground, dirt covering his face. "And what is that?"

"To see death and stay alive." She cups his cheeks. "Open your eyes. Open them, son of Enoch. You have years of life in you, but if you do not accept death, you cannot accept life. So, watch me. Watch me and accept it. Only then can you live."

My chest hurts. I start crawling toward him as much as I can, but I'm too weak to make it very far.

Cassius runs over and picks me up, then whispers in my ear, "Trust us."

I shake my head. "He's mine."

"So let him choose," he says right back. "Just like the stars. And just like you did so many centuries ago."

I can't watch, so I turn my head when Tarek opens his eyes and locks gazes with Medusa.

I'm too afraid to look.

Cassius sets me down. A hand grabs mine, and I glance left. It's Genesis. She smiles and squeezes my fingers. "Remember, fear is not welcome here."

"Not welcome," Stephanie adds.

"Never," Hope agrees.

Before I know what's happening, all the women walk with me toward Tarek, and I see him stand, completely alive and whole.

I run toward him.

But something stops me.

"You," a childlike voice says, "and I need to talk."

My entire body freezes as I turn and look at the Creator. "Are you here to end me?"

"Why would I end the beginning?" He smiles and holds out his hand. He looks maybe sixteen, then changes into a man in his thirties of Arabic descent, then an Indigenous person, then a woman of Jewish ancestry. "Why would I ever end my Creation?"

Chapter Sixteen

Tarek

I feel fine, but I need her. I need to touch her.

Instead, all I see is her staring at me, and everyone surrounding us. I know that I was healed. I know I'm fine, but I'm exhausted. Danu is gone, but my person is still here, still on this Earth, my Earth. I need her.

I reach out with shaking hands.

"Shhh." Mason, my brother, pulls me into his arms then dusts me off. "Man, you're a mess. Just gotta be so dramatic about everything. The apple returned to its spot beneath the Earth, and so did Danu. And look at you." He shakes his head. "Hot mess."

Horus sighs and pulls his leather jacket tighter across his shoulders. "He really was dramatic, just lying on the ground."

"All done." Timber walks up and dusts off his hands. "She's in the Underworld but not in the nice, safe place. More like the 'oh, look, torture,' up top." He holds his hand up for a high five while all the angels remain standing around us in formation. "What? Too soon?"

I hit his hand because it's almost embarrassing—he's been holding it up for longer than a few seconds—then watch the Creator talk to Lilith.

They're so many things.

A man. A woman. Of every descent. Every face. They encompass all things, and it's incredible to watch it happen, like They want everyone in the universe to know.

I am.

I am all things.

I am you.

You are me.

You have a purpose.

And you are not alone.

Lilith falls to her knees and raises her hands, and we all watch with the angelic army as hundreds of stars shoot through the skies.

They lean down and kiss her cheek. Clothed in red robes covering both face and body, They walk away, join the army, and nod Their head.

The legion pulls out their swords, and before They leave, They look to Cassius and smile. "Well done."

"Good," Timber whispers. "And faithful."

Horus finishes. "Servant."

"Do you think," Mason asks, "that they realize that phrase came from Gilgamesh, or should we not reveal that?"

"Ever," Stephanie adds.

Cassius says, "No. That would confuse everyone way too much. All they need to know, all *humanity* needs to know, is that we aren't going anywhere. And, apparently...the first female of this Earth is going to marry her werewolf, technically the oldest part human in existence."

I crack a smile. "Is that why my knees hurt?"

Horus smacks me on the back while Timber laughs.

"Let's go." Cassius jerks his chin toward me, his black hair falling down to his waist. He looks terrifying, but that's normal for him. His eyes match his hair, and purple feathers push out of his back, extending into a wingspan that's at least twelve feet across, if not more. "I think you deserve a drink."

"Thank you." I lower my head. "For finding us. For saving us."

"Saving?" Cassius questions. "We didn't come here to save you; we came here to support you. As you said very eloquently, the world doesn't always need a savior, they need a sacrifice. Someone willing to give their all to save just one." He pats me on the back and walks away.

Chapter Seventeen

Lilith

I don't even know how to describe how the last few days have been. I still have the star inside me—Cassius said her sacrifice was her choice. And Tarek...well Tarek's been sleeping, trying to recover.

I grab another bottle of juice and some crackers and walk upstairs. The room is silent. I knock a few times, then shove the door open when he doesn't answer.

He's lying in bed like he's dead.

He has no clothes on, just a small part of the duvet covering his thigh. His gorgeous dark hair falls around his chin, touching his shoulders, and his full lips are pulled into a pout as if he's upset.

I briefly put my hand under his nose to make sure he's breathing, only to have him snatch me by the wrist and tug me against his warm body. "It's not fair that I get the smell of you but no bites. What did They tell you?" His eyes open, so bright and clear. "What did the Creator tell you?"

I swallow slowly, my face pressed against Tarek's chest. "They told me to live. They..." Tears well in my eyes. "They set me free."

"And the punishment of two days to roam the Earth? Gone?"

I smile sadly. "All because one of the oldest humans to live is in your blood. Only because an apple of the Fallen was returned to its source. All because—at one point—you loved me, and I loved you back. And when it really mattered, when you put your life on the line for another, it showed mercy. So, you see, your bravery mattered, as well as your sacrifice. You talk about saving others, knowing their futures, not knowing your own, not being needed by anyone because of your gift, but in the end, you saved me every time without even knowing it. I owe you everything. My gratitude, my love, my heart, and my soul."

Tarek goes very still.

I start to get up, but he pulls me right back down, pinning my body against the soft bed. "Not so fast."

I inhale his scent. He's still so delicious, like the very air I breathe and the earth I walk on. "Why not? Don't you need rest?"

Tarek pushes me harder against the mattress, his smirk sending chills down my spine as my legs move to get away from him. "Oh, hell no. I need respite."

"And how does that happen?"

"I believe you sucked on me a few days ago." His smirk has me feeling so many things that I'm almost afraid to speak. His smile spreads wide as he grips me by the neck and throws me against the mattress. "Maybe now it's my turn."

Panic hits me, and then he cups my face. "I'll sacrifice for you. I'll kill. I'll do anything. But, Lilith, what I won't do is ever force you. So know that while I want nothing more than to torture you the way you did me… I'll go back to sleep and pretend this moment never happened if you want." He leans down and presses a kiss to my cheek, then whispers in my ear, "But I really want to bite."

Chills run down my spine as I look into his now-blue eyes, they flash gold briefly. It's beautiful. I watch his full lips turn red in anticipation and his fangs elongate. I slowly turn my head so he sees my vein. "Then, by all means, werewolf. Bite."

His fangs dig into my neck before I can scream, and ecstasy washes over me instantly. Warm blood drips down, and he feeds so hard I feel his fangs digging past my vein. I feel him in my soul.

There is no escaping his grip, no freeing myself from his trap.

It's like the sun burning me from the inside, yet I want more. I grip the back of his neck and pull him closer. "More," I whisper.

"Always." He flips me onto my back and rips my shirt from my body, then the rest of my clothes. "Always." He flips me over and draws his claws down my back, creating wounds that will scar and stay there for an eternity, ones he'll lick with his tongue, ones I'll beg for again and again.

After all, blood is life. And I am life. So is he—beginning and end.

His tongue heals the scratches.

I almost beg for more.

I understood werewolves used blood. I knew it, but I'm not prepared when his bites go from my neck down to my ass, and then he digs in before pulling back and thrusting into me with such force that I *know* he's claiming me.

"Finally," he rasps, moving his hips against me. "Finally. Finally."

"Finally," I moan and look over my shoulder.

He shakes his head, his eyes closed, and jaw clenched. "Mate. Finally." His eyes suddenly flash open, and they're glowing blue then gold then blue again. "Finally. You."

I can't stop my scream as he drills into me, and my body flushes with heat, pleasure, and everything else all at once. He is mine. I am his. I dig my fingers into the mattress when he collapses against me and moves slower, like his fever dream is over, and only ecstasy remains as he holds me close.

Cradled in his arms.

I feel treasured.

He kisses my neck, my back, and sighs against me with tiny breaths that have goose bumps erupting all over my back.

"Mine." I can barely hear him.

And then I feel it as he releases.

And I orgasm.

I feel it as I turn and see a tear running down his cheek. It's silver, and I want to touch it. It's so beautiful.

It's solid, like ice. I shake my head. "So, you do hold the stars, don't you, werewolf?"

He nods. "Prince of the Earth. And I kind of have a best friend who's God of the Sky…but this isn't for me."

I frown. "What?"

Still connected, still inside me, he reaches his hand up and pulls the tear from his cheek, placing it on my lips. "It's for my mate. May the Creator bond us forever. May the stars shine. And one day"—he smiles—"this star will grow, a final gift from the one who sacrificed."

"A gift?"

He smiles and kisses me, then brushes his lips against my mouth. "A star chooses to fall and can be reborn. Did you think her sacrifice was for nothing? One day, we'll have a star of our own. A child. A parting gift. Because blood must always be shed but must also be reborn, daughter of the Creator, Lilith, the first… And you will not be the last."

Epilogue

Tarek

I stare at the tiny baby in my arms and try not to cry. Mason slaps me on the back. "So, you finally became a man. Good for you."

"Hilarious, but why is she so small?" I ask.

He grins. "Well, as a Fallen Angel and half werewolf, I can honestly tell you, you know secrets from the stars, but when they choose to fall, it's for a purpose. So, in your case, she knew." He nods and pats me again. "She knew what you would do. And my guess? She's been watching for thousands of years, just waiting." A tear escapes his eye.

"Bro, are you crying?" Alex runs up. "Is the baby okay? Stupid hospital is being all like: '*We don't let the likes of you in here.*'"

We both stare him down.

He's literally half-naked.

"A shirt." Timber runs up behind him. "People need them when in public places, dumbass."

Cassius suddenly walks up, his cell to an ear. "Yeah, baby is fine. Everything is good. Apocalypse solved."

Ethan follows him, furiously texting. "I swear if I have one more poopy diaper…" He stares at the baby, then at me, and grins. "Have fun, though. Really. I'm rooting for you. Fighting."

Horus isn't any better as he slowly walks in and yawns. "Life is so hard in the modern world. My air fryer sucks. Oh, hey, a baby."

My child immediately starts to cry. But it's the most beautiful wail I've ever heard. She's gorgeous and looks like her mother with dark hair, light eyes, and a small scar that looks like a star on her chest.

"So, what's her name?" Bannik walks up.

We haven't seen him since that day with Danu. He's in modern clothing, a black leather jacket, ripped jeans, and a T-shirt that says, *Ain't life grand?*

And Medusa is hooded by his side. They're holding hands. I feel so much joy coming from them that I almost can't contain mine. "I don't know."

Bannik laughs, his black hair whipping across his back as he approaches and grabs the baby from my arms without me even offering.

He lifts her to his face.

The Fallen of the Fallen.

The one angel who nearly destroyed us all over his bitterness, sadness, and need for revenge. One who once stood at the feet of the Creator.

He turns and holds her close. "Ah, yes. You are special. It's good you know."

"She talks?" Cassius whispers under his breath.

Bannik presses a kiss to my daughter's cheek and starts speaking in the angelic tongue. It sounds like another language to anyone but those touched by the Earth and Heaven.

"Shaddaih, El, Ni, hear me now. Gods. Universe. Goddesses. For this blessing, beautiful daughter, what an honor. You will do great things. The grace of the Creator is the gift for your sacrifice. How lucky we are to have you on this Earth to help guide us. The Creator has never failed and won't stop now. I call upon every star in Creation to guide you and every angel to watch you, because that is what we do. We watch, and we always will. You are ours, and we are yours."

He turns and hands me back my child. "And now she has a name."

"What?" I look down at the sweet, precious girl and see a small glimmer on her chest next to the star.

Tears pour down my eyes as I read what's there. "Moriah."

Sacrifice in Hebrew.

The sacrifice.

Mine, her mother's, the star's, all of ours—in order to keep everything balanced.

Cassius wraps an arm around me. "It's good."

"It's perfect," I answer and look up at my new family, wondering to myself what I ever did to deserve them, my wife, or any of this.

As we're all talking and some are walking away, I see Them in the background.

The Creator.

A small child smiles at me, Their eyes glistening as They whisper,

"It's good. It always will be."

I nod.

They nod back.

And then They're gone like They never existed.

"It's good," I repeat and kiss Moriah's face, knowing I need to bring her back to her mom to rest.

Then I watch them thrive. I watch them live.

It's wonderful, really, when you think about it. Lilith, the first, finally has *her* first.

A child born out of sacrifice, love, and the stars that watched us for so long.

I smile as I look up at my family again. "Life is hard, isn't it?"

"Very." Cassius smiles at me, and his eyes flash. "But there is always purpose in our struggle. Because out of that struggle…" He looks down and whispers as he touches my daughter's head. "Comes life."

* * * *

Also from 1001 Dark Nights and Rachel Van Dyken, discover Mafia King, Provoke, Abandon, All Stars Fall, Envy, and The Anti-Fan and the Idol.

Sign up for the 1001 Dark Nights Newsletter
and be entered to win a Tiffany Key necklace.

There's a contest every month!

Go to www.1001DarkNights.com to subscribe.

**As a bonus, all subscribers can download
FIVE FREE exclusive books!**

Discover 1001 Dark Nights Collection Ten

DRAGON LOVER by Donna Grant
A Dragon Kings Novella

KEEPING YOU by Aurora Rose Reynolds
An Until Him/Her Novella

HAPPILY EVER NEVER by Carrie Ann Ryan
A Montgomery Ink Legacy Novella

DESTINED FOR ME by Corinne Michaels
A Come Back for Me/Say You'll Stay Crossover

MADAM ALANA by Audrey Carlan
A Marriage Auction Novella

DIRTY FILTHY BILLIONAIRE by Laurelin Paige
A Dirty Universe Novella

HIDE AND SEEK by Laura Kaye
A Blasphemy Novella

TANGLED WITH YOU by J. Kenner
A Stark Security Novella

TEMPTED by Lexi Blake
A Masters and Mercenaries Novella

THE DANDELION DIARY by Devney Perry
A Maysen Jar Novella

CHERRY LANE by Kristen Proby
A Huckleberry Bay Novella

THE GRAVE ROBBER by Darynda Jones
A Charley Davidson Novella

CRY OF THE BANSHEE by Heather Graham
A Krewe of Hunters Novella

DARKEST NEED by Rachel Van Dyken
A Dark Ones Novella

CHRISTMAS IN CAPE MAY by Jennifer Probst
A Sunshine Sisters Novella

A VAMPIRE'S MATE by Rebecca Zanetti
A Dark Protectors/Rebels Novella

WHERE IT BEGINS by Helena Hunting
A Pucked Novella

Also from Blue Box Press

THE MARRIAGE AUCTION by Audrey Carlan
Book One
Book Two
Book Three
Book Four

THE JEWELER OF STOLEN DREAMS by M.J. Rose

SAPPHIRE STORM by Christopher Rice writing as C. Travis Rice
A Sapphire Cove Novel

ATLAS: THE STORY OF PA SALT by Lucinda Riley and Harry
Whittaker

LOVE ON THE BYLINE by Xio Axelrod
A Plays and Players Novel

A SOUL OF ASH AND BLOOD by Jennifer L. Armentrout
A Blood and Ash Novel

START US UP by Lexi Blake
A Park Avenue Promise Novel

FIGHTING THE PULL by Kristen Ashley
A River Rain Novel

A FIRE IN THE FLESH by Jennifer L. Armentrout
A Flesh and Fire Novel

Discover More Rachel Van Dyken

Mafia King: A Mafia Royals Novella

One of the first rules they give you when you're undercover—never fall for the enemy.

I didn't just fall for the enemy.

I became what I was supposed to hate.

What's worse: I fell in love with one.

I live a double life, and both sides know it's only a matter of time before I'm forced to choose.

Rebirth through mafia blood.

Or death at the hands of the very government I swore to protect.

I have one more job before my time's up.

I just wish it was anything but babysitting a mafia princess who's half my size but knows how to pack such a brutal punch I worry about my ability to have children.

Tin's small but terrifying.

And I'm her new bodyguard while we all go on a much-needed vacation.

I just have to stick to the plan.

And remember rule number one.

And stop kissing her.

* * * *

Provoke: A Seaside Pictures Novella

The music industry called me a savant at age sixteen when I uploaded my first video and gained instant fame. And then Drew Amherst of Adrenaline became my mentor, and my career took off.

Everything was great.

Until tragedy struck, and I wondered if I'd ever be able to perform again. I fought back, but all it took was a falling light to bring it all back to the fore. So, I walked away. Because I knew it wasn't just stage fright. It was so much more.

The only problem?

Drew and the guys are counting on me. If I can't combat the

crippling anxiety threatening to kill me, I might lose more than I ever dreamed of.

Enter Piper Rayne, life coach, with her bullshit about empowerment, rainbows, and butterflies. She smiles all the damn time, and I'm ninety-nine percent sure there's not a problem she can't solve.

Until me.

She was given twenty-one days to fix me. To make me see what's important. What's real. The problem is, all I can see now is her. The sexy woman who pushes me. Provokes me.

Only time will tell if she's able to do her job—and I can make her mine.

* * * *

Abandon: A Seaside Pictures Novella

It's not every day you're slapped on stage by two different women you've been dating for the last year.

I know what you're thinking. What sort of ballsy woman gets on stage and slaps a rockstar? Does nobody have self-control anymore? It may have been the talk of the Grammys.

Oh, yeah, forgot to mention that. I, Ty Cuban, was taken down by two psychotic women in front of the entire world. Lucky for us the audience thought it was part of the breakup song my band and I had just finished performing. I was thirty-three, hardly ready to settle down.

Except now it's getting forced on me. Seaside, Oregon. My bandmates were more than happy to settle down, dig their roots into the sand, and start popping out kids. Meanwhile I was still enjoying life.

Until now. Until my forced hiatus teaching freaking guitar lessons at the local studio for the next two months. Part of my punishment, do something for the community while I think deep thoughts about all my life choices.

Sixty days of hell.

It doesn't help that the other volunteer is a past flame that literally looks at me as if I've sold my soul to the devil. She has the voice of an angel and looks to kill—I would know, because she looks ready to kill me every second of every day. I broke her heart when we were on tour together a decade ago.

I'm ready to put the past behind us. She's ready to run me over with her car then stand on top of it and strum her guitar with glee.

Sixty days. I can do anything for sixty days. Including making the sexy Von Abigail fall for me all over again. This time for good.

Damn, maybe there's something in the water.

✦ ✦ ✦ ✦

All Stars Fall: A Seaside Pictures/Big Sky Novella

She *left*.

Two words I can't really get out of my head.

She left *us*.

Three more words that make it that much worse.

Three being another word I can't seem to wrap my mind around.

Three kids under the age of six, and she left because she missed it. Because her dream had never been to have a family, no, her dream had been to marry a rockstar and live the high life.

Moving my recording studio to Seaside Oregon seems like the best idea in the world right now especially since Seaside Oregon has turned into the place for celebrities to stay and raise families in between touring and producing. It would be lucrative to make the move, but I'm doing it for my kids because they need normal, they deserve normal. And me? Well, I just need a break and help, that too. I need a sitter and fast. Someone who won't flip me off when I ask them to sign an Iron Clad NDA, someone who won't sell our pictures to the press, and most of all? Someone who looks absolutely nothing like my ex-wife.

He's tall.

That was my first instinct when I saw the notorious Trevor Wood, drummer for the rock band Adrenaline, in the local coffee shop. He ordered a tall black coffee which made me smirk, and five minutes later I somehow agreed to interview for a nanny position. I couldn't help it; the smaller one had gum stuck in her hair while the eldest was standing on his feet and asking where babies came from. He looked so pathetic, so damn sexy and pathetic that rather than be star-struck, I took pity. I knew though; I knew the minute I signed that NDA, the minute our fingers brushed and my body became insanely aware of how close he was—I was in dangerous territory, I just didn't know how dangerous until it was too late. Until I fell for the star and realized that no matter how high they are in the sky—they're still human and fall just as hard.

* * * *

Envy: An Eagle Elite Novella

Every family has rules, the mafia just has more....

Do not speak to the bosses unless spoken to.

Do not make eye contact unless you want to die.

And above all else, do not fall in love.

Renee Cassani's future is set.

Her betrothal is set.

Her life, after nannying for the five families for the summer, is set.

Somebody should have told Vic Colezan that.

He's a man who doesn't take no for an answer.

And he only wants one thing.

Her.

Somebody should have told Renee that her bodyguard needed as much discipline as the kids she was nannying.

Good thing Vic has a firm hand.

* * * *

The Anti-Fan and the Idol: A My Summer In Seoul Novella

Make it or break it...

Or maybe just break them?

Ai-Ri has been training under YK Management in Korea for two years without any results. She doesn't fit the typical mold for a successful K-POP idol image, literally down to her blood type. She has six more months before college entrance exams which means she only has six months to make it as an idol before her dreams are crushed.

Things take a turn when two of the most famous male idols break away from their group and decide to form their own co-ed group, a rarity.

And wonder of all wonders, they need one more girl.

It would be the perfect opportunity, except she hates them.

They are arrogant, entitled, rich little snobs who want the world to worship the ground they walk on. To make matters worse, the only reason they came to her was because they are desperate, which means she needs to prove herself even more.

Tempers and personalities collide when she's forced to either accept the position or give up on her dream.

But what happens when you suddenly go from anti-fan and enemy number one to stuck in a love triangle between two boys you were born to hate but are somehow falling in love with? And will the group survive the heartbreak that follows when she finally makes her choice?

Exposing the Groom
By Rachel Van Dyken
Now Available!

Killian swept in like a knight in shining leather pants to save Scarlett once she *exposed* the groom. The next time they saw each other, they ended up fake-engaged. Can they find a way to make it down the aisle together and live happily ever after? Find out in #1 *New York Times* bestselling author Rachel Van Dyken's EXposing the Groom, a romantic comedy with a side of rockstar.

How it started:
An accidental phone grab during my rehearsal dinner while my fiancé went to use the restroom.

How it ended:
Reading all the dirty texts between him and my maid of honor, aka little sister, during our vows in front of the world in what would later be considered one of the most viral wedding videos on TikTok.

Of. All. Time.

Did I mention his vows were before mine, and he compared me to my adopted dog because... and I quote, "I'm so loyal."

It's not my fault that my first instinct, after exposing his dirty lies, was to run up to the clueless rockstar that was supposed to headline my reception and ask him to sing my tears away. I never expected him to help me escape certain disaster, kiss me senseless, and then buy me ice cream.

But that was all in the past—until I'm staring down at a wedding invitation from the crappy little crap pants ex. You see, he swapped sisters, and now a year later, they're getting married at a gorgeous winery while I'm still staring down at a plus one, wondering if I can bring my pet turtle.

How it happened:
In desperation, I sent a drunken text to the hot rockstar with a picture of my turtle, Chuck Norris... in a bowtie. Who knew he would show up at the wedding—but get this, it wasn't to save me, nope, it was to... yup, SING!

SHE STOLE HIM TOO!

But now that he's there and I'm there, and the history is there, I beg him one more time to save me, this time as my date.

But lie after lie just kept pouring out of my mouth until we were somehow fake-engaged.

I would laugh if crying didn't feel so good.

Should have brought the freaking turtle...

* * * *

"Who gives this woman?" The priest asks. He has no idea what sort of hell I'm about to unleash, it almost makes me laugh.

"Her mother and I." My dad says proudly.

Rob comes over and reaches for my hand as we walk up to the altar. He even shakes my dads hand, with both of his hands as if to show that he's this dominate thing when he's literally afraid of taking me against a wall.

Idiot.

I'm suddenly more angry.

I planned for this moment.

I hold the paper in my left hand, I crumple it, and as we go through the ceremony and get ready to say our vows, Rob turns to me.

"I think about you every day, Scar." His eyes tear up. "You're my everything, you're perfect, my best friend, everything I've looked for in a life partner. Remember the time we adopted that dog with the missing leg and you said that sometimes you feel like somethings missing on you? I think that something was me, I'm that something, we complete each other—"

The actual hell is he comparing me to a dog? My favorite dog that I will sick on him if he doesn't stop talking.

"—You're my little Bun Bun."

And he just called me our shared dogs name.

At our wedding.

In front of five hundred friends.

"—So friendly, so willing to do anything to please, and so kind to everyone you meet. I feel like that's where our story started, and this is where it ends, with forever, us together forever. All because of Bun Bun."

He must have seen something like murder flicker in my eyes because he momentarily drops my hands and then picks them up again. "I love you."

I grit my teeth.

"Scarlett?" The priest looks to me. "You can read your vows now."

"Can I face the audience? It's really important they understand the depth of my love for Rob." I smile sweetly.

"Oh wonderful! What a blessing for everyone in attendance!" The priest clasps his hands together like he's about to say a prayer of thanks, when I turn from Rob and smile at the crowd.

Everyone's smiling right back like aw, happy moment, do your thing! Oh. I. Will.

I unfold the small paper and start to read.

"Rob," I look towards him quickly. "This is for you. These words, while so meaningful, really helped change my life so I want to say thank you for being so transparent…"

He frowns and then says. "That's beautiful, thank you—"

"—Damn, I wish my fiancé knew how to act in bed." I just keep reading. "You're so hot, don't worry, I'll figure something out, she's just a wife, she's not like a mistress, you're so hot, so sexy, can you come over tonight? Let me send you a dick pick I know you love those, though lets be honest it doesn't even fit in the phone, haha."

I keep reading even though Rob reaches for me.

I jerk away from him.

"She doesn't know, come on, she majored in communications, you don't even need college textbooks to ace those classes, plus she looks good and people love her, she never even argues with me. Why do you think I like your backbone? You should come over, she's gone for the next hour." Tears stream down my cheeks. "No I changed the sheets." My voice cracks. "She'll never know you were even here, I even told the maid." I choke up. "My mom knows, she caught me texting you on the other phone, but don't worry, baby, baby, I'll break up with her once we're together for a bit and say she wasn't who I thought she was, then I'll marry you, my true love." I start sobbing. "My one and only love." I shake. "My little Addison."

My. Little. Sister.

I drop the paper onto the floor and turn to him. His face is pale, his mom's crying, his dad looks ready to murder him.

I shake my head, I can't even say any words, so I turn back towards the crowd, hold my head high and say. "Let's not waste a good party, I'll be at the reception drinking, oh and Addison…" I glare at my sister. "Your grooms waiting."

I don't look back.

I walk with my head held high straight to the bar at the reception, order a double, and then I sit and watch the band start to play.

The singers famous.

He's beautiful.

They're still doing a soundcheck.

I toss back my drink and walk towards him, stopping right in front of the stage.

He looks up at me. "Aren't you supposed to be getting married?"

"Sing me a song." I say, and then I burst into tears.

And that's how I went viral.

Not from my vows, which were spectacularly captured on Tik-Tok, but because I begged one of biggest singers in the world to sing.

And he did.

About Rachel Van Dyken

Rachel Van Dyken is the #1 New York Times, Wall Street Journal, and USA Today bestselling author of over 90 books ranging from contemporary romance to paranormal. With over four million copies sold, she's been featured in Forbes, US Weekly, and USA Today. Her books have been translated in more than 15 countries. She was one of the first romance authors to have a Kindle in Motion book through Amazon publishing and continues to strive to be on the cutting edge of the reader experience. She keeps her home in the Pacific Northwest with her husband, adorable sons, naked cat, and lazy dog.

You can connect with her on Facebook:
www.facebook.com/rachelvandyken
or join her fan group Rachel's New Rockin Readers:
https://www.facebook.com/groups/RRRFanClub.

For more information, visit her website at:
http://rachelvandykenauthor.com

Discover 1001 Dark Nights

Paige ~ CLOSER by Kylie Scott ~ SOMETHING JUST LIKE THIS by Jennifer Probst ~ BLOOD NIGHT by Heather Graham ~ TWIST OF FATE by Jill Shalvis ~ MORE THAN PLEASURE YOU by Shayla Black ~ WONDER WITH ME by Kristen Proby ~ THE DARKEST ASSASSIN by Gena Showalter

COLLECTION SEVEN
THE BISHOP by Skye Warren ~ TAKEN WITH YOU by Carrie Ann Ryan ~ DRAGON LOST by Donna Grant ~ SEXY LOVE by Carly Phillips ~ PROVOKE by Rachel Van Dyken ~ RAFE by Sawyer Bennett ~ THE NAUGHTY PRINCESS by Claire Contreras ~ THE GRAVEYARD SHIFT by Darynda Jones ~ CHARMED by Lexi Blake ~ SACRIFICE OF DARKNESS by Alexandra Ivy ~ THE QUEEN by Jen Armentrout ~ BEGIN AGAIN by Jennifer Probst ~ VIXEN by Rebecca Zanetti ~ SLASH by Laurelin Paige ~ THE DEAD HEAT OF SUMMER by Heather Graham ~ WILD FIRE by Kristen Ashley ~ MORE THAN PROTECT YOU by Shayla Black ~ LOVE SONG by Kylie Scott ~ CHERISH ME by J. Kenner ~ SHINE WITH ME by Kristen Proby

COLLECTION EIGHT
DRAGON REVEALED by Donna Grant ~ CAPTURED IN INK by Carrie Ann Ryan ~ SECURING JANE by Susan Stoker ~ WILD WIND by Kristen Ashley ~ DARE TO TEASE by Carly Phillips ~ VAMPIRE by Rebecca Zanetti ~ MAFIA KING by Rachel Van Dyken ~ THE GRAVEDIGGER'S SON by Darynda Jones ~ FINALE by Skye Warren ~ MEMORIES OF YOU by J. Kenner ~ SLAYED BY DARKNESS by Alexandra Ivy ~ TREASURED by Lexi Blake ~ THE DAREDEVIL by Dylan Allen ~ BOND OF DESTINY by Larissa Ione ~ MORE THAN POSSESS YOU by Shayla Black ~ HAUNTED HOUSE by Heather Graham ~ MAN FOR ME by Laurelin Paige ~ THE RHYTHM METHOD by Kylie Scott ~ JONAH BENNETT by Tijan ~ CHANGE WITH ME by Kristen Proby ~ THE DARKEST DESTINY by Gena Showalter

COLLECTION NINE
DRAGON UNBOUND by Donna Grant ~ NOTHING BUT INK by Carrie Ann Ryan ~ THE MASTERMIND by Dylan Allen ~ JUST ONE WISH by Carly Phillips ~ BEHIND CLOSED DOORS by Skye Warren

~ GOSSAMER IN THE DARKNESS by Kristen Ashley ~ THE CLOSE-UP by Kennedy Ryan ~ DELIGHTED by Lexi Blake ~ THE GRAVESIDE BAR AND GRILL by Darynda Jones ~ THE ANTI-FAN AND THE IDOL by Rachel Van Dyken ~ CHARMED BY YOU by J. Kenner ~ DESCEND TO DARKNESS by Heather Graham~ BOND OF PASSION by Larissa Ione ~ JUST WHAT I NEEDED by Kylie Scott

Discover Blue Box Press
TAME ME by J. Kenner ~ TEMPT ME by J. Kenner ~ DAMIEN by J. Kenner ~ TEASE ME by J. Kenner ~ REAPER by Larissa Ione ~ THE SURRENDER GATE by Christopher Rice ~ SERVICING THE TARGET by Cherise Sinclair ~ THE LAKE OF LEARNING by Steve Berry and M.J. Rose ~ THE MUSEUM OF MYSTERIES by Steve Berry and M.J. Rose ~ TEASE ME by J. Kenner ~ FROM BLOOD AND ASH by Jennifer L. Armentrout ~ QUEEN MOVE by Kennedy Ryan ~ THE HOUSE OF LONG AGO by Steve Berry and M.J. Rose ~ THE BUTTERFLY ROOM by Lucinda Riley ~ A KINGDOM OF FLESH AND FIRE by Jennifer L. Armentrout ~ THE LAST TIARA by M.J. Rose ~ THE CROWN OF GILDED BONES by Jennifer L. Armentrout ~ THE MISSING SISTER by Lucinda Riley ~ THE END OF FOREVER by Steve Berry and M.J. Rose ~ THE STEAL by C. W. Gortner and M.J. Rose ~ CHASING SERENITY by Kristen Ashley ~ A SHADOW IN THE EMBER by Jennifer L. Armentrout ~ THE BAIT by C.W. Gortner and M.J. Rose ~ THE FASHION ORPHANS by Randy Susan Meyers and M.J. Rose ~ TAKING THE LEAP by Kristen Ashley ~ SAPPHIRE SUNSET by Christopher Rice writing C. Travis Rice ~ THE WAR OF TWO QUEENS by Jennifer L. Armentrout ~ THE MURDERS AT FLEAT HOUSE by Lucinda Riley ~ THE HEIST by C.W. Gortner and M.J. Rose ~ SAPPHIRE SPRING by Christopher Rice writing as C. Travis Rice ~ MAKING THE MATCH by Kristen Ashley ~ A LIGHT IN THE FLAME by Jennifer L.

On Behalf of 1001 Dark Nights,

Liz Berry, M.J. Rose, and Jillian Stein would like to thank ~

Steve Berry
Doug Scofield
Benjamin Stein
Kim Guidroz
Chelle Olson
Tanaka Kangara
Asha Hossain
Chris Graham
Jessica Saunders
Stacey Tardif
Dylan Stockton
Kate Boggs
Richard Blake
and Simon Lipskar

Made in the USA
Columbia, SC
03 November 2023

25403668R00069